D0684048

The Aftermath

a novel by
Anna J.

Q-Boro Books
WWW.QBOROBOOKS.COM

An Urban Entertainment Company.

L3531983
East Baton Rouge Parish Library
Baton Rouge, Louisiana

Published by Q-Boro Books
Copyright © 2006 by Anna J.

All rights reserved. Without limiting the rights under copyright reserved above. No part of this book may be reproduced, stored in or introduced into a retrieval system, or transmitted, in any form, or by any means (electronic, mechanical, photocopying, recording, or otherwise), without prior written consent from both the author, and publisher Q-BORO BOOKS, except brief quotes used in reviews.

ISBN 0-9776247-4-9
First Printing September 2006

20 19 18 17 16 15 14 13 12 11

This is a work of fiction. It is not meant to depict, portray or represent any particular real persons. All the characters, incidents and dialogues are the products of the author's imagination and are not to be construed as real. Any references or similarities to actual events, entities, real people, living or dead, or to real locales are intended to give the novel a sense of reality. Any similarity in other names, characters, entities, places and incidents is entirely coincidental.

Cover Copyright © 2006 by Q-BORO BOOKS all rights reserved
Cover Layout & Design—Marion Designs
Editors—Pittershawn Palmer, Melissa Forbes, Tee C. Royal, Candace K. Cottrell

Q-BORO BOOKS
Jamaica, Queens NY 11431
WWW.QBOROBOOKS.COM

The Aftermath

Dedication

In memory of those I hold close to my heart, I dedicate this book to:

Juanita T. Pitts
Sunrise October 15, 1923—Sunset April 8, 2004

Nancy A.C. Rich
Sunrise October 5, 1954—Sunset April 28, 2005

Herbert S.S. Forrest, Sr.
Sunrise April 3, 1936—Sunset August 3, 2005

Harry E. Pitts
Sunrise January 11, 1951—Sunset December 28, 2005

Thanks for looking out for me up there . . . I miss you.

Acknowledgments

First giving honor to God through whom all blessings flow, thank you for giving me the ability to complete yet another novel, and if it be your will may I complete many more.

Mom, Paul & Tiffany thanks so much for all of your support. You guys helped me out so much with the promotion and tours for *My Woman His Wife*. Traye and Tiffany, thanks for passing out bookmarks at my signings. Paul, Thanks for all of the books you sold on the job, and for just spreading the word. Mom, thanks for all of the support and for all of the books you helped me sell.

Aunt Karen, girl what can I say? You have been my rock for so long. Thank you so much for the talks and for keeping my hair looking fly. No matter what time of day I called with concerns you always made time to hear me out and offer me good solutions. You have a way of letting me know that my "problems" aren't as bad as I think they are. I love you so much for just being you, and I wish you all the best in everything you do.

Aunt Sandy, thanks for everything. You held me down too, and it's greatly appreciated.

Tisha and Shar, y'all have been my girls and favorite cousins since day one. Thanks for loving me, y'all! Tisha, me and you grew up more like sisters, so you know how we roll. Shar, keep doing the dang thing, I'm proud of you. And if anyone doesn't believe we related, tell them to call me. (LOL)

Naquan Bryant, where would I be if I didn't know you? Thanks for being there to help me when I didn't think I had anybody to turn to. You've helped me so much in my quest to maintain my spirituality, and you've brought things to light that have been on the dark for way too long. I love you for that. Thanks for everything.

Eugene Riley, how long has it been? Ten or twelve years now? True friends are hard to come by, and I'm glad you're one of them. I wish I could give you the man of the decade award. Not too many men are willing to step up to the plate and take care of kids that don't belong to him like you did. You will be blessed for that, and they're coming soon. Trust me. ☺

Ken Divine, as always it is a pleasure. I wish you all of the luck in the world with your next book. August can't get here fast enough. Thanks for always giving me a place to lay my head when I visit the Big Apple, and for just being a true friend to me.

Mark Anthony, we did it again! Thank you for having faith in me and trusting that I can do this. You taught me so much about the industry and restored my faith in knowing that there are good people out there who are willing to blow me up and not put me down.

To my QBB Family—Eric, and Kiniesha. What better place for talented writers to gather than Q-Boro Books? Mark knew he had a winning team when he signed us on. Thank y'all for so much love and support. I wish each of you all the success in the world with your novels. Let's put QBB on the map! To everyone else who just signed on, welcome to the QBB family. And to all those haters out there who didn't see us coming, we write those hot books. You didn't know?

Nakea Murray, girl you had me getting my travel on for that first book! Thanks for you help in putting my book on the map, and showing me a side of the industry I never knew existed. Books don't always sell themselves, so thanks for having my face in every place possible.

T.L. Gardner, my biggest supporter. How I wish I had the imagination you possess. You are such a talented writer, and believe me when I tell you that when you finally show your face the world is going to love you. You're going to be huge one day, and when you do make it to the top don't forget about us little people. Welcome to the Q-Boro Family. ☺

Blair Poole, I am so proud of you!!! *Breathe* is gonna knock 'em dead. I hope you sell a million books and write a million more. You have truly been a good friend, and I'm so glad we met.

Kimber Lee, thanks for everything. I can't wait for your book to hit the scenes, girl. The world ain't ready for you. You have been wonderful in holding down PWP, and as hectic as my life is sometimes, you have always been a reason for me to slow down and breathe a little bit. I wish you and Ray a lifetime of love and happiness, and hurry up and get that book finished!

Angie, the hottest hairstylist on this side of West Philly. You're doing big things at Primp & Pamper. Thank you for telling all of your clients about my book and for holding me down like you do. You've been styling my hair since I was in the 9th grade! Thanks for keeping me fly over the years, and I wish you much success in everything you do.

Marlene Ricketts, Thanks for remembering me when you were trying to get your book right. I wish you continued success, and thanks for spreading the word about me in your area. Keep writing those hot books; you're on your way to the top!

Wendy Jenkins-Ross, we had an instant friendship from the first day we met. I see big things happening for you with your book and your restaurant business, and I wish you all the success your heart and hands can hold.

To my girls at Captivating Styles, Dorthea, Jada, Dominique, and Kim. Keep doing y'all thing over there. Dorthea, thanks for letting me come up in there and get that paper. Dom, congrats on your new baby, and good luck with your schooling. Jada and Kim, much love to y'all and keep tossing them heads up.

Diane Dancey of Sequins Fashions, what can I say? You gave me my first shot at modeling and a chance to show the world that being big can most certainly be beautiful. Keep doing what you do best: making America sexy one stitch at a time. When I get on *Oprah* you know I'll need an outfit. Work your magic!

As The Page Turns Book Club, thank y'all for everything. Pashen, I owe you the world for riding out with me and taking me to book signings outside of Philly. You were always down for a road trip, no questions asked. As a whole, every last member has been there for me unconditionally. Trish, hurry up and get that book out!

To every member of the Philadelphia Writers Partnership, all of you made writing this and every attempt at writing so much easier. A group of such talented writers of all genres deserves recognition. The world ain't ready for y'all. I wish you speed and creativity in getting your books out, and an extra push in getting over any writers block that may be hindering you at the moment. I want to be able to walk into a bookstore and see your names on the shelves. Let's make it happen!

To all my people from BlackThoughtz.com, thank y'all so much for your support. Y'all made sure to get my book when it came out, and showed me so much love whenever I came to the MD area. Shawan -aka- Ms. Loochie For Sho'! Keep doing ya thing, ma. Your site is so on point.

To my people from coast2coastreaders.com, thanks for all the love and support and I'll be looking for y'all at the Harlem Book Fair!

Last, but certainly not least, thank you to every one who purchased *My Woman His Wife*. Y'all showed me love at every book signing and event and by purchasing online. A writer is nothing without a reader, so I am nothing without you. Thanks for the love, enjoy your book, and be sure to spread the word!

—*Anna J.*

Through Monica's Eyes: Three Months Ago

"I knew you when I had a friend. Very deeply love lived within, But somehow we got loose from what was oh so tight. Somewhere we went wrong when we were oh so right..."

"Hello?"

"Monica, it's Sheila."

"Just the person I wanted to hear from. What's good with you?"

"I've been calling you all week. Why haven't you returned my calls?"

Sheila was getting on my last nerve with all the questions. Didn't she know I was the one who asked the questions around here? My first instinct was to snap, but I finally had James where I wanted him and I needed her help.

"I've been extra busy, sweetie. I'm sure you understand. I'm so glad you called."

"Why are you glad, Monica?"

"James is coming here later. We can do what we talked about."

"Well, I have a better idea."

I held the phone back and looked at it for a second. Was she trying to tell me what to do, and since when did she get a damn backbone? I detected a little frustration in her voice, but I decided to ignore it. I had shit to do.

"What could be better than what I came up with? We both know who the mastermind is on this team, Sheila."

"If it were you, you would have Jazz by now, right?" Sheila asked as though she was interrogating me.

I have to admit I was speechless, but I heard her out. Apparently, the happy couple was now walking on a rocky road. This was perfect, because James couldn't function under pressure and it would be that much easier to talk him into coming to my house.

"He seemed frustrated at the gas station this morning. He also confirmed that he would definitely be over later. He is absolutely hating Jazz right now," I said.

"Monica, I'm telling you it would be better if we did it at their house. What woman wouldn't freak out over that?"

"Yeah, but what if she snaps on all of us? That would defeat the purpose."

The goal was to have Jasmine mad at James, not at me. If I walked into my house and saw my mate in that position everyone would be dead. No questions asked. But Sheila was making it sound like her idea was a good one, and maybe she was right. Jazz would hate James for sure, and I'd be there to comfort her. Yeah, that would be perfect.

"How will I get him there? He doesn't want his wife to know he's cheating, idiot."

"It's simple. All you have to do is . . ."

I listened as she shared this entire story about having my house fumigated so we couldn't use my spot. It sounded stupid enough to work. However, I wasn't so sure. James wasn't the brightest bulb on the tree, but he wasn't the dimmest either. At the end of the day, his family mattered most.

"And if he doesn't go for it?" I asked Sheila. For the first time I was doubting myself.

"It'll work. You know how to get shit done."

"What time should we be at the house?"

"We should be in the house getting it on by six. She'll be there no later than six thirty. I'll meet you there and . . ."

Sheila told me to keep the door unlocked so she could walk right in without James actually having to answer the door. By then we should already be having sex. She would just join in. All I knew was if her ass didn't show up, she'd have serious issues later; mark my words.

"Sounds flawless. Talk to you later," I said. I was hoping our plan would work, but I'd be lying if I said I didn't have doubts.

"Monica, one more thing. I need you to call your man at the ticket office. I need two courtside seats for the married couple for tomorrow night."

"Done. Anything else?"

"What's James's favorite food?"

"Caribbean. We always order from this place called A Taste of the Islands that's near their house." I wasn't sure what Sheila had in mind, but I would help her with whatever she needed to pull this thing off.

"OK, that sounds perfect."

"Anything else?"

"Don't be late," Sheila commanded.

After we hung up I went to soak in a nice, long bath, making sure to scrub my entire body until my skin glistened like warm cinnamon. I had recently made a trip to The Body Shop, so I opted to massage the mango body butter I just purchased into my already soft skin.

I refreshed my toenail polish for good measure, then slipped into a pale pink dress that barely covered my ass. I put on James's favorite pair of stiletto sandals that strapped up to mid-calf. Looking at the clock, I knew James would arrive soon, so I made my way downstairs and posted by the window until I saw his car pull up.

I was already outside and moving toward his car before he

turned the ignition off. His face looked sad as I attempted to hug him, but I acted like I didn't notice. I needed to be at his house within a half hour, and I didn't have time to play.

"Hey sweetie, I missed you," I said while trying to wrap my arm around his neck. He stopped me and took a step back, then looked into his car. I glanced over to see his son sleeping and his daughter staring at me before putting her head back down.

"I can't stay. I forgot I had to pick up my kids from school. Can I make it up to you tomorrow?"

"I'm leaving town tonight. Why can't we do it tonight?" I pouted and crossed my arms over my chest. I couldn't take no for an answer. Too much was at stake.

"I just told you why. Why can't I see you when you get back?"

"Because I want you now. I can follow you to the house and come in after you put the kids down for a nap. Come on, James, I need you today."

"What if Jazz comes home and catches us? Then what?"

"Have we ever gotten caught before?" I was starting to get pissed. This dude had been hittin' it all this time, and now he wanted to get a conscience? Give me a damn break.

"No, but now could be the time."

"James, come on with the bullshit. Are we doing this or what?"

"Look, just follow behind me and wait until I tell you to come in."

I didn't say a word as I reached behind my door to grab my keys. I hurried to lock the door as James walked back to his car. I then hopped in my strawberry colored Expedition to follow him home. Instead of parking in front of the door when we got there, I parked a few houses down.

I was getting anxious as time ticked on. I thought James was trying to play me, and just as I moved to go knock on the door, I saw him calling me into the house from the window.

By then it was already six o'clock and Sheila was pulling up as I was walking up the street. I glanced her way briefly before entering the house, leaving the door unlocked for her.

I found James in the kitchen drinking a soda and looking scared as hell. I took the bottle out of his hand and placed it on the counter. I walked him around to the other side of the table and began undressing him, sitting him in the chair so his back was to the door. I took my dress off and draped it on the chair next to us.

After taking his dick into my hands I felt it pulsate as I placed wet kisses up the underside of his long, chocolate stick before circling the head with my tongue and placing it in my mouth. I rotated between deep-throating him and going halfway down as if he were fucking my pussy instead of my mouth. One hand massaged his testicles while the other slipped up and down his shaft, causing his mouth to drop open and his eyes to roll to the back of his head. Just as he was about to cum, I stopped, telling him to hold it as I prepared myself to ride him.

James melted instantly as I squeezed my walls around his length, almost causing him to ejaculate prematurely. I moved slowly up and down on him as his arms wrapped tightly around my back. I pushed my nipples together, placing them up to his lips. He didn't hesitate to open his mouth and bless them with his tongue. I bounced harder and faster, only slowing down when he was about to cum.

I saw Sheila enter the house and close the door behind her. To keep him distracted until she got closer, I tightened my walls around him. When he opened his eyes, Sheila was standing right next to us. She looked like she didn't know whether she wanted to stay or leave, but she quickly made up her mind after seeing the look on my face. She knew if she even thought about leaving I would be on her ass, and the expression on my face said just that.

She stripped naked and climbed up on the table. I turned

around to face her, never getting off James's dick. I continued to ride him as I began tasting Sheila. Spreading her lips
apart with my thumb and forefinger, I took her clit into my
mouth and stroked her with my tongue to the same rhythm
James was stroking my clit with his finger. Periodically, I
would stick my tongue inside of her before going back to
teasing her clit. I didn't hear when the door opened. The
next thing I knew, I heard Jasmine's voice.

"What the fuck is going on here?"

James practically threw me off him, but I felt him cum before he had a chance to get me off him completely. Sheila
fell off the side of the table and crawled underneath it. I
smirked a little and said nothing as I let James explain for all
of us.

"Jasmine, what are you doing home so early?" James asked
her in a frightened tone. I was thinking she was right on
time as I watched him try to cover up his erection with a
damn potholder. I wanted to go over to Jasmine's side, but I
was naked too.

"What the fuck is going on here? Where are my kids?"

"The kids are cool. Just calm down. It's not how it looks."

I looked at him like he was crazy. What did he mean it wasn't
how it looked? We were fucking on her table! I wanted to
smack him in the back of his head for saying that stupid shit,
but I refrained for the time being.

"Where are my kids, James? This is my last time asking
you!"

I could see that Jazz tried to stay as calm as possible in this
situation, but her anger level was quickly rising on the
charts. If she didn't get an answer soon, all hell would break
loose. James was standing there looking like he was about to
shit on himself, and I was starting to feel scared my damn
self. Jazz was on the verge of snapping, and the look in her
eyes told me she had checked out of reality a long time ago.

"They're upstairs. They should be sleeping. Please, just stay calm and—"

"You had a threesome in my kitchen with my secretary and my friend on my brand new table and you want me to stay calm? My fuckin' kids are in this house, and you want me to stay calm?"

I was enjoying the show. James kept digging a deeper hole for himself. Looking back at Jazz, I went from enjoying the scene to being scared as hell. This bitch spazzed the fuck out and started throwing knives and shit. I jumped behind the table after she threw the first knife so my ass wouldn't get cut. Jazz had the snaps, and for the first time I felt bad. I fucked up her happy home, but what could I do now?

"Jazz, fall back. Why you trippin'?" I managed.

She didn't answer. She just kept throwing knives. I mean, who actually had that many? She had to have thrown at least fifty of them, and they were still coming.

"Jasmine, please let me explain," Sheila spewed out of nowhere. I wanted to punch her in her throat for bringing Jazz's attention to us under the table. She was doing perfectly fine trying to chop James's ass into little pieces, and now this bitch got her focused on us. At that point I just wanted to get out alive.

Jazz stopped and looked at all of us for what felt like an eternity. I kept my damn mouth shut and looked at her, wondering how I would make this right. She took one last look around the kitchen before she dropped the knives she had in her hand and ran out of the kitchen, I'm sure to get her children.

I jumped up to put my clothes on, and James and Sheila followed suit. By the time we got dressed and moved to the living room, Jazz was down the steps and on her way out the door. I decided I would wait until she left to let James know my secret.

"Jasmine, you just can't leave like this. Can we talk?" he pleaded.

Jazz gave him the look of death. I had to turn my head because the pain in her eyes was unbearable. Sheila looked like she was going to piss on herself. I hated her right then. Listening to her dumb ass got us into this shit, and I would make her pay dearly. Jazz continued to secure her children in their car seats before jumping into the driver's seat and pulling off. James stood at the door and watched her until we could no longer see the taillights on her car.

James slammed the door and we started arguing about the situation. I saw Sheila slip out the back door. I would get her ass soon, but I just had to tell James what was going on.

"James, I'm pregnant."

"By who?"

"By who? I'm pregnant by you. It's your child!"

"Monica, you need to get the fuck out of my house. I don't need any more shit out of you, and if you *are* pregnant, then get rid of it."

"But, James, I thought you wanted me!"

"This is my last time asking you to leave. Next time I'll snatch you by your neck and throw you out. Now go!" he said angrily.

I decided not to argue. Quickly grabbing my shoes and keys, I left. I fell into a heap of tears when I got home. I would make this right. If I didn't do anything else, I would make this right.

We now return you to your regularly scheduled program already in progress . . .

Jasmine D. Cinque

At one point in my life I thought I had everything under control. I ate my vegetables, pleased my husband, looked after my children, and went to work every day. No one told me that one day you could look up and your life would be a disaster. My momma never told me to beware of marital mishaps and conniving women. I thought if I did everything right the first time and kept everyone happy, I would be blessed with a marriage like the one my mother and father had.

Shit, they'd been married for thirty-six years and I couldn't ever remember the silent treatment being passed between them. Even when I look at them now, they appear to be in love as much as they were when they first laid eyes on each other, if not more. Why couldn't I have that?

I felt like someone had ripped my heart out with their bare hands. The only thing that gave me the will to live was my children. I gave that bastard everything, and this was how it turned out for me? Every time I looked at my son I saw James, and I couldn't help but cry. One day my son would be some woman's husband. Would he break her heart the way his father did mine? Or would my poor little girl reap the sins of her father?

Every time I looked in the mirror I wondered what had happened. Years ago, I saw a smart businesswoman with nothing to lose and everything to gain. At the age of thirty-seven I could still drop it like it was hot with the younger crowd and "Electric Slide" with people my own age. I was a tigress in the bedroom, living room, garage, and anywhere else my husband decided to be creative. But as I looked in the mirror, all I saw was a woman scorned, and I didn't know how to fix it.

Yes, I was partly to blame since I had agreed to let another woman enter the sex life of me and my husband. But so what? I mean, just because I agreed to it, does that mean I deserved to be totally disrespected and humiliated? I don't think so.

Like I said, I didn't know how to fix my jumbled feelings, but one thing I did know was that I was fully capable of medicating my feelings of scorn and bitterness.

The way I saw things, I figured what better way to medicate my feelings than to flip the script by allowing myself to indulge in some freaky and disrespectful sexual behavior the same way my husband had done by violating our kitchen with those whores!

Ever since the day of that ugly and unfortunate episode that I had witnessed taking place in my kitchen, I had not been able to get the picture of my husband screwing two other chicks out my head. It was like I could see the whole incident replaying itself in slow motion. I can even remember the smell of sex that was in the air that day, and no matter what I do, I can't seem to shake that smell or dislodge that thought from my mind.

The only thing that seemed to work was when I found myself in Bally's working out, running on the treadmill or something. And since James and I had been apart, I found myself visiting the gym regularly, at least four times a week. I would go to the gym after work to get my mind off things.

In fact it was at Bally's where I decided to hatch my plan

for vindication. Not total vindication, but vindication that would leave me feeling somewhat satisfied.

There were these male twins who I'd met at the gym. Things developed from an informal hello-how-are-you-doing type of relationship to a more casual, us talking about our workdays type of relationship. In between there was always a bunch of flirting on their part, but I never paid it any mind.

That was then, but now that I had found myself not as happy in my marriage, I decided to indulge in their flirtatious ways.

I called over to one of the twins, "Hey Donnie, can you spot me?" I asked, while lying on my back getting ready to do incline bench presses.

"Jasmine?" Donnie asked with a question mark in his voice. "What you know about bench pressing? Incline at that?"

"Well I know that it's the best thing to keep my tits from sagging." I said while totally catching Donnie off guard.

Donnie laughed.

"Come on, I gotchu," he stated as he lifted the forty-five pound bar off the rack and helped me get my workout on.

Before long Donnie's twin brother Rahmel walked over to where the two of us were and began talking.

"So you only doing one set?" Donnie asked while also informing Rahmel that I was doing bench presses to keep my tits from sagging.

"Say word?" Rahmel stated as he began laughing.

I could have continued on with the conversation going in that direction, but to be honest, my plan was already hatched in my head and I was ready to set it in motion.

"You know what, I always see the two of you whenever I work out and I have been meaning to ask one of y'all for the longest time if you do personal training."

Donnie and his brother looked at each other and they smiled.

"Yeah, we do. Why?" Rahmel asked with a sinister smile on his face.

"Because I'm looking for someone to train me. I mean, the gym is good and all, but I have a gym and equipment in my house and I know I could get in better shape if I had someone to stay on top of me and keep me in line."

"So you're saying you want a personal trainer to come by your crib and train you?" Donnie asked.

"Yes, that's what I'm saying."

There was a brief awkward pause.

"Well it's not that serious. I mean . . ."

Donnie cut me off by smiling and saying, "No, I gotta keep it real with you. We workout, but as far as personally training somebody, we ain't no personal trainers or nothing like that."

"Well, that's ok. Like I was getting ready to say, it's really not that serious, meaning I really just need somebody to come by the crib just to keep me motivated. I know y'all can help motivate a sister, right?" I said while adjusting the drawstring on my spandex workout pants.

Donnie and his brother agreed to both personally train me. We never spoke about price or anything like that, yet they agreed to come by my house on that upcoming Friday morning. They both would be free since they worked the graveyard shift, so they had no problem committing to the time.

I, on the other hand, knew that I had to finagle some things in order to free up my time, especially considering I was planning on having the twins show up at my house. See, I had walked out on James and was staying with my brother, so I didn't know what James's schedule would be like on Friday morning. I didn't know if he would be home or not, but since he worked 9 to 5 I figured he would be at work and that I would be ok.

Still, the thing was James and I didn't have a lick of workout equipment in our house and that was OK, because in spite of the wedding rings I noticed on Donnie and his brother's hands, I was determined to get it on with both of them. I don't know if Monica's ways had rubbed off on me or what, but in my desire to medicate my bitter feelings, I was willing to stoop to the level of getting it on in a three-some with two men, married men at that.

The way I looked at it was James had totally disrespected me by bringing two women into my kitchen and fucking them while my kids were in the house, so why couldn't I bring two men into my house and get it on in with them at the same time in the same kitchen?

When Friday morning rolled around I had made it to my house and James wasn't home. I figured he had left for work. It felt eerie walking into my own house and as soon as I walked in, those scenes of Monica and Sheila sexing my husband instantly came back and gripped me. It was at that point that I decided not to even step foot into my kitchen because it would bring back too many memories.

I entered the living room and for a brief moment I contemplated what I was planning on doing with the two unsuspecting twins when they arrived. And I figured I could get one up on James by bringing them right into the same bedroom that James and I once shared.

Before I could give it much more thought, my doorbell rang and it was the twins.

Taking one last look around the room, and solidifying my decision to use the bedroom, I put on a brave face and opened the door without asking who it was. I mean, who else could it be at that time of morning?

"Hello, fellas. Thanks for coming through." I smiled as I stood back to let them in, suddenly happy I opted to wear the shortest skirt I owned with no panties underneath. I wanted this to be as easy and quick as possible.

The twins looked puzzled at first, and I'm sure they were wondering why I didn't have any workout gear on. After locking the front door, I signaled them to follow me up the stairs.

"Follow me, fellas. The workout room is this way."

I took the liberty of walking ahead of them on the steps, making sure to give them a good view of my bare ass. I had gone to get a Brazillian wax the other day just to ensure that the entry would be smooth. I didn't look back to see if they followed, and used the sound of their boot clad feet hitting the steps as indication that they were close behind.

Opening the door to the room James and I shared up until the recent events, I entered and stood in the middle of the floor, watching their faces to see what they were thinking. Just as I thought, Donnie was the first to speak.

"Jasmine, what's all this about? You said you wanted us to help you train. I don't see any exercise equipment in here." He nervously looked at his brother, then to the bed, and then back at me. A wicked smile spread across my face as the thought of getting back at James rang like sweet revenge in my ear. To ease Donnie's mind I walked closer to him and stood breast to chest, noticing his quickening breath as I ran my fingers down his arm.

"There's exercise equipment in here, sweetie. Big enough for all of us to work out at the same time."

Backing up slowly, I began to strip out of the skirt and shirt I had on and placed my naked body in the middle of the bed for display. Opening my legs wide, I spread my lower lips apart and inserted my middle finger into my wetness, working it in and out for a few seconds before taking that very same finger and putting it into my mouth and sucking it clean of my own juices.

Donnie and Rahmel were still standing in the same spot with looks of shock on their identical faces. Rahmel looked like he was ready to get it on, while Donnie, on the other hand, didn't look like he was too sure about going through with it.

I continued to please myself, allowing soft moans to escape my lips, hopefully enticing them to join me. Donnie was the first to take his wedding band off and undress, placing his face between my legs. Rahmel stood watching us for a while, not sure what he wanted to do.

Donnie flipped me over with ease, entering from the back and pounding me with long, hard strokes that made my breasts bounce against my stomach and caused my breath to escape from my lungs. Not long after, I saw Rahmel's naked form on the side of the bed, and I didn't hesitate to grab his dick and place it inside of my warm mouth. I had yet to see what Donnie was working with, but from the feel of it these guys were really identical from head to toe.

Rahmel was ready to join in the fun and signaled for his brother to let up so he could lie on the bed. After he got comfortable, I straddled his length and after a few strokes I paused for a quick second so Donnie could enter me through the back door. We moved like synchronized swimmers, our collective moans sounding like a swarm of honey bees. By the time I came down on my fifth stroke, Rahmel had come inside me, but my constant movement kept him from going down.

We switched from one position to the next, and at one point both men were standing in front of me while I gave one head and one a hand job until they both came all over my face and neck. I had to lay on the bed and get myself together after that workout, but the fellas quickly dressed and headed out, promising to meet me at the gym later that day.

I didn't even bother to change the bed linens, I just merely fixed it back to the way it was, threw the clothes I had on in the dirty laundry hamper, and proceeded to the shower. My nipples and clit were still warm and a little tender from the work Donnie and Rahmel put on me, and I smiled while I got dressed in an outfit from my closet and made my way out, happy to enjoy the rest of my day.

James D. Cinque

Where did I go wrong? The Creator gave me everything I had ever asked for. I was on top of my game. Most men envied me. I climbed the corporate ladder quickly and remained humble when I reached the top. I had it all. I was given a wonderful woman who loved me unconditionally, and the blessings kept coming when we found out Jazz would be having twins. But as I looked at my reflection in the mirror, I had to wonder what the hell went wrong.

Thinking with my "other" head was what went wrong, but could you blame me? Monica wasn't just any woman. The girl had to have put a root on me or something, because not in all the years I'd been married had I allowed anyone to interfere with my relationship with my wife. The little flings I had on the side were kept under control, and Jasmine never knew about them. Somehow Monica turned the tables and messed up everything. Not only did I not have my wife, but I'd gotten another woman—who I didn't even want anything to do with—pregnant.

I was surprised when Jasmine's brothers didn't come

banging my door down waving guns. I wanted them to because there was no way I deserved to live after all that. Hell, I already felt dead inside, so they may as well have taken my body. Maybe I needed to suffer, because even though I was going through a horrible time, I could only imagine how my wife was feeling. And that damn Sheila . . . that one really surprised me. I guess Monica had us all under her spell.

All I knew was that I needed to get my home back in order, and I needed to do so as smoothly as possible. The transition wouldn't be pretty, but I was more than willing to take the risk. I couldn't breathe without my babies, and I needed to hold my wife in my arms. If I got another chance I swore I'd make it right, but for now I figured I'd start by purchasing a new kitchen table because that would be one less thing she had to deal with if she came back home. I didn't even feel right eating meals there myself, so how could I expect her and my kids to?

Yeah, I wanted to do right by my wife and the new kitchen table would be a small start. But I knew that if I really wanted to do right I would have to do a complete 180 when it came to the way I thought about sex. I mean, sex sort of dominated my mind and my life. To me it was like everything I saw in certain porno movies I felt like I had to live it out. But it was just something about the threesome thing that really just had a vice on me. I craved it and I needed it like a crackhead needs crack.

While Jasmine and the babies were at her brother's house, I knew that that was the time I had to use to just focus and get myself right, but at the same time I sort of felt the freedom of a bachelor. And that freedom was something I hadn't felt in a long, long, long, time.

I knew I had been wrong by letting myself get too wrapped up with Monica from an emotional standpoint and I would never make that mistake again.

With my newfound freedom I decided to take one more stab at the threesome thing just so I could finally get it out of my system.

I had met some bangin' strippers who worked at The Cat House. The Cat House strip club was a spot I had began to visit just about every night since Jasmine and I were apart. And while I was always respectful to the different dancers I met at the club, I was also always upfront and very candid with them as well when I would proposition them for sex.

Like I said, I had learned from the Monica episode, so with the strippers I met, my approach and MO was always the same; cash for that ass. I wasn't interested in any emotional connection or involvement. The strippers had what I wanted in the form of ass, and I had what they wanted in the form of cash.

And it wasn't long after I began visiting The Cat House that I had found more than a few ready and willing sexual participants who had agreed to hook up with me at my house to make the exchange of cash for sex.

There were two chicks in particular who I'd arranged to meet at my house. One was a black chick named Desire and the other one was a Spanish chick named Ina. Both were into the girl on girl thing, which for me was a must.

Earlier in the week I already had it set up for Ina and Desire to meet me at the crib at eight o'clock. I was showered and smelling fresh in a silk robe with nothing under it. They arrived right on time, and we didn't waste any precious minutes making small talk. They were there to get paid and laid, and then they could move on.

Once we entered the bedroom, Desire removed my robe and instructed me to lie on the bed. I did as I was told, and tried to control the smile spreading across my face as the two women danced and grinded on each other in front of me.

Ina was the color of hot cocoa, and Desire was the color of cocoa when wet. They looked delicious together. Where Ina had a nice round ass that most women of Spanish descent were known for, Desire was blessed with the most beautiful set of breasts, with nipples that looked like they were dipped in dark chocolate. My man stood at attention just thinking about the possibilities.

As the music played the women kissed and touched each other, and I watched through eyes at half mast with my right hand working my strength. Ina came and laid down on her back between my legs with half her body hanging off the bed. Desire mounted her so her pussy sat right on Ina's mouth, and she rode her tongue while she swallowed me whole. The rhythmic motion of her head bobbing up and down, and the feel of her mouth as she blew down on my dick and clamped her jaws tight on the way up made me come all in her mouth, and she sucked me back into an erection in no time.

Desire's body shook with release shortly after mine, and Ina moved from under her to a position behind, spreading her ass cheeks and making her face disappear from my view as she tongue fucked Desire in the ass. I just sat back and let them work for their money.

Switching positions, Ina got up from behind Desire, and after sliding a mango colored condom on me, in an anal entry she began riding me while Desire got comfortable between her legs. She switched from eating Ina to juggling my balls in her mouth. The grip Ina's ass had on me was beyond words, and soon after, I busted my second nut of the night.

Ina removed the condom and tossed it in a small bag they placed on the dresser. The idea was for them to never leave any evidence behind, so they took everything with them when they left. Used condoms and all.

Desire put another condom on me after working me up into the ready position. She rode me and Ina sat on my face. The two women fed from each others' breasts until we all exploded in a simultaneous climax. That shit was off the damn chain.

I allowed the ladies to clean up and we had a little more fun in the shower before they had to go. As promised, I paid their fee for the night in cash, and saw them to the door. I waited until they were in their car before I locked up and turned in for the night. The last thing I heard before drifting off to sleep was the night time newscaster from T.U.N.N. telling viewers to get ready for the nine day forecast. If what just went down didn't get a threesome out of my system, I didn't know what would.

Monica L. Tyler

What had I become? I just knew I had everything on lock, but somehow I messed up along the way. I was supposed to be a part of a happy family. Jasmine, her children, and I were supposed to be filling the space under my roof. I had succeeded in getting pregnant, so James was no longer an issue. For the life of me I just couldn't put my finger on where I had messed up.

And that damn Sheila! Lord knew I didn't want to talk about her. She said her plan was foolproof. Why in the hell did I listen to her? I mean, what woman wouldn't be mad if she walked into a threesome on her kitchen table? I was surprised Jasmine didn't cut us all up into little pieces. I honestly think the only thing that saved us were the kids being in the house.

I wanted to call James to see if he had a number for Jasmine, but I knew he wouldn't cooperate. I had to find a way to get around things and get back into his good graces. Maybe now that Jasmine wasn't an issue, he and I could hook up. Shit, who was I kidding? That man wanted me dead and his unborn child with me. If only I could just get him to listen to reason . . .

I had a doctor's appointment the following Monday, and I was hoping she'd tell me something good. I've tried carrying before, and it didn't work out, so I was hoping this pregnancy would be followed all the way through and the baby would be born healthy. I was also wondering if she could tell me about the nightmares I'd been having. I thought all of that had stopped once I got out of my uncle's hellhole, which was cleverly disguised as a house. My head pounded just thinking about it, and I couldn't even take anything because I was knocked up.

Well, one thing I could say was that I'd never been a quitter. I hoped if I could just talk to Jasmine she'd see things my way. As I looked at myself through my mirror, I hoped what I saw was still appealing to her.

I would wonder about Jasmine on a daily basis and although I wasn't physically with her, that didn't stop me from being connected to Jasmine and being *with* her in my mind. In fact, on almost a nightly basis I would masturbate while fantasizing about being with Jasmine.

My routine and my fantasy was pretty predictable. Each night I would begin by lighting my candle and placing my favorite song, "Reunion," on repeat before making myself comfortable in my bed. "Reunion" was the first song I heard as I watched Jasmine and James dance on the night we met. The very night I fell in love with her.

I started out with my little silver bullet like always. I lifted my legs up and back so that my knees touched my ears, and my pelvis pointed towards the ceiling. In a slow circle, I started with the vibrating tool on low and traced my erect clit in small circles. The closer I got to my orgasm the more I increased the speed of the bullet, every so often dipping it into the puddle of juice that was quickly collecting at my opening. By the time I reached my climax my body would be shaking from the currents of pleasure running through my body.

I would imagine my tongue was Jasmine's as I placed my nipples into my mouth and fingered my clit until the shaking subsided enough for me to grab Hector, my ten-inch, hot pink dildo from the table. I always started out with slow strokes so I could tighten my pussy muscles around the shaft, making it almost difficult to pull it out. I would close my eyes, picture Jasmine's naked body in my mind, and start fucking myself harder and faster pretending I was doing it to Jazz until I squirted my love juice all over my sheets.

To finish it off I grabbed the Jackrabbit, a beaded vibrator that had a rotating head and beads that jumped around on the inside, causing all kinds of havoc. On the outside the little bunny ears rested on your clit, and once turned on, they squeezed and vibrated on your clit in conjunction with the inside action, causing my damn head to spin.

By the end of the night I was thoroughly fucked, but missing Jazz even more. I knew I couldn't have her to myself, but if I could just get her one last time . . .

Jasmine

Taking Baby Steps

"**M**ommy! Mommy!" my four-year-old twins screamed at me in unison while shaking my sleeping body. It felt like I had just fallen asleep, my eyes dry as a bone from all the tears I'd shed. It'd been about three-and-a-half months since the catastrophe at my house, and I still couldn't seem to get it together.

"Don't y'all see Mommy is trying to sleep?" I asked as I reluctantly opened my eyes to acknowledge them. My daughter gave her brother an "I told you so" look as she brushed her long braids away from her face.

"Mommy, are we going to see Daddy today?" my son asked, oblivious to the stares both his sister and I were giving him. I felt so bad because they had been asking me that same question every day since we came to my brother Dave's house.

It was killing me on the inside because they were too young to understand. It wasn't that I was keeping them away from James, but if I saw him at that time I may have ended up behind bars. Although he could have called to check on them himself, he made no moves to see about their well-being, and that pissed me off. For the first three weeks he called every day, pleading with my brother to get me on the phone. My brother said he was going to stay out of it, but I knew he wanted to go hurt James for the pain he had caused his little sister.

"Let Mommy get herself together, and I'll let you know in a bit, OK?" I said to them as I swung my legs around to the side of the bed so I could get up. I'd been feeling nauseous all week and the light-headedness was a bit much. I didn't even want to entertain the thought of being pregnant again. Not then anyway.

"OK, Mommy," my twins said in unison before kissing me on my cheeks and walking away.

I sat there on the side of the bed for a second trying to figure out my approach. I wasn't ready to see James yet, but our kids were having a hard time dealing with the separation. Well, Jalil was. Jaden just seemed to go with the flow. She was the stronger one. I contemplated what I would say as I reached over and picked up the receiver. Dialing the number was painful as I thought about what had happened under that roof, but I had to do it for my children. I slowed my breathing as my heart pumped at top speed in my chest. I maintained my cool when I heard his voice. James answered on the third ring.

"Hello?" James's voice sounded a millions miles away to my ears. The man I loved with all of my heart and soul, the man who had hurt me the most.

"Hey, James, it's me," I said into the receiver. I could hear his breathing quicken at the surprise of hearing me through the other line.

"Jasmine, baby, I'm so sorry," he began, his voice sounding like he was holding back tears. I was struggling with my own tears as I finished with the call, making it as quick as possible.

"I was calling to see what you were doing this afternoon.

The kids have been asking for you a lot. Maybe we can stop by." I kept it cool although I wanted to curse his ass out for doing me the way he did.

"Sure, please do. I miss all of you so much. Can we talk when you get here, please?"

"Only if we're talking about the kids, James. I'm not ready to relive that horror right now."

"Jazz, please don't be like this. I made a mistake, baby. Just give me a chance to redeem myself, please," James begged from the other end of the phone connection. He started sounding hysterical and a part of me really didn't give a damn. I wanted him to suffer. We definitely needed to talk, but I was not in the mood.

"James, right now I just want to bring the kids by to see you. We can talk when they're not around. Now is not the time."

"Jazz, listen to me. I want you to bring the kids, but is it possible you can get your brother to watch them tonight? Jazz, please, I can't live like this anymore."

"You should have thought about that when . . ." I couldn't even finish the thought. Pointing the finger at him would be pointing three back at me. I had to admit that I fell for Monica's bullshit, but I wasn't ready to take the blame yet. We had both messed up, but he got caught.

"Jazz, please just think about it. You can bring the kids now if you want, but I need you to come back tonight. I'm begging you, please give us a chance at starting over. I can't breathe without you and my kids."

"James," I began, letting out a long sigh in an attempt to keep my tears in check. We did need to air out our dirty laundry, so why was I procrastinating? "I'll be there in about an hour. I have to get the kids washed and dressed, OK?"

"Can we talk tonight, Jazz? Please?"

"I'll be there in an hour, James." I hung up before he could say anything else.

This was going to kill me, but I had to face him. I missed him so much and I didn't want our kids to suffer because of our problems, but I couldn't seem to get up the nerve to make things right. He had hurt me terribly. As I pulled out clothes for us to wear, thoughts ran through my head a mile a minute. There was so much I wanted to discuss, and I contemplated leaving the kids so we could say what we had to say, but I knew they wouldn't let me leave the house without having a fit.

I washed myself, then them, and got all of us ready. We piled into the jeep, leaving a note for my brother on the fridge. Making the trek across town from Mount Airy to Wyncote felt a lot longer than the half hour it was. The block seemed a mile longer than it did when I was under that roof. I blasted my Tupac CD all the way to the front door, keeping my head up just as the rapper suggested.

Before I was even out the car, James was out the house and unbuckling Jaden from her car seat. I avoided eye contact as I un-strapped Jalil and placed him on the ground so he could give his Daddy a hug. James looked like he was close to tears as he hugged our kids close to him, their little arms barely fitting around his neck. I stood back, taking in the scene and wondered why our family couldn't always be as perfect as it seemed at that moment.

We finally made eye contact, but I looked away first, keeping my tears in check as I walked around him and went into the house. As soon as I stepped in, it felt like all the oxygen had left the room as flashes of that night raced through my mind. I could still smell the food I purchased that night. Shaking off the dreary feeling, I removed my jacket, then turned to remove Jaden's. Jalil was already out of his and back in James's arms.

I wanted to have a seat, but I felt restless. I wanted to jump on his damn neck and bash his head in for being stupid enough to get caught. I too was guilty of playing on Monica's field, but damn. Why did it have to end this way? I knew she wanted me for herself, and at one point in time I was considering it, but in reality there was no way possible I would have left James to be with her. I'd been loving him for too long.

Before I had a chance to sit, James pulled me into the kitchen. That was the last place I wanted to be. That bitch was parked on my kitchen table like she had a right to be there. This meeting was going way too fast, and I was ready to take my kids and make a hasty retreat. Entering the kitchen I was pleasantly surprised to see that the table had been replaced. In its place was another set that was a lot more expensive than the one I ended up purchasing. Ten cool points for James for making this a little easier. This gesture didn't make me forget the events that happened here, but at least we didn't have to endure the pain of dining on the same set that they used to have their freak fest. But at the same time I knew that I was one to talk because I had fucked two guys right upstairs in our bedroom. But, hey, at least I was smart enough to not get caught!

There was a spread fit to feed ten people. Our feast was set up as if we were at a picnic. All of us took our normal seats while James served us before taking his food. I didn't want to look at him, but I did notice he was looking mighty tasty in his crisp, white wife-beater and button-down shirt. His body looked more buff in his jeans, making my panties wet just thinking about the power underneath. He sported a fresh cut, his goatee and side burns lined perfectly. The smell of his Cool Water cologne was driving me crazy, but I chilled. It wasn't that kind of party.

We ate in silence . . . well, I did. James kept up a lively conversation with the kids as they gave him blow by blow of the weeks spent at their uncle's house. I sat in silence and let him have his time with them. Every time I looked up I could feel his eyes on me, but I pretended it didn't bother me. He wanted to see his kids, and I had granted him his request. I didn't want it to be said that I was trying to keep them away from him.

Jalil chatted away; he was so happy to see his dad. Jaden looked occupied by her own thoughts, playing more with her food than actually eating it. I wondered if my baby girl felt what was going on between her parents. She was definitely a daddy's girl, but lately she'd been kind of withdrawn.

We finished up and went to sit on the back patio so the kids could play on the swings and seesaw we had built to match their clubhouse. The neighbor's children were outside, so they were too happy to see their friends. I sat on the lounge chair opposite James so I could have a good view of the kids. They looked so happy and carefree as they raced up and down the slide and around the yard. I remembered similar days and longed for life to be that simple again.

For a while James stayed in his seat across from me, staring directly at me. I knew he wanted to talk, but I wouldn't be the one to initiate the conversation. I honestly didn't want to talk about it with the kids there, just in case I wanted to use a few choice words to get my point across. At the same time I wanted nothing more than for him to hold me in his arms and make the pain go away. I wanted to be a family again.

James got up and sat next to me, draping his arm across my shoulder, my head finding a place to rest on his shoulder out of habit. Nothing made sense to me at that moment. I still wanted to be mad at him for what happened, but I loved him so much I honestly couldn't stay upset forever. It felt good being in his arms, his chin resting on top of my head, his breathing like a lullaby. I closed my eyes and breathed in the scent of my man, wrapping my arms around his waist in comfort.

"Jazz, I'm so sorry things ended up this way," James began as we cuddled on the patio. My eyes remained closed as I listened to his words. His voice sounded deeper with my head pressed against his chest.

"James, can we talk about this later?" I wanted to talk, but I knew right then wouldn't be a good time.

I wanted to enjoy the moment before it got tense again. He breathed a long sigh, and his grip tightened around me. I held on to him like my life depended on it as I watched the kids play, so innocent at that age. Jaden was the bossy one and Jalil was a natural born leader. I smiled on the inside at what I was able to bring into the world. As hectic as my life had been lately, when I looked at our children they reminded me that peace still existed on this twisted planet we call home.

James put his finger under my chin, lifting my face up to meet his. At first I thought he was going to kiss me, and I wouldn't have resisted. To my surprise he just stared at me, tears threatening to fall from his pretty brown eyes. I wanted to put his soul at ease and let him know everything was OK, but we both knew it wasn't.

"Jazz, I know I messed up, baby. Just know that I love you more than life itself and I'll do whatever I have to do to make this right. I know you don't want to talk right now and I respect that. I just want you to know that I need you in my life. I need my children, and I need us to be a family again. I love you, Jazz, I really do. Can we please just work this out? I feel like I'm suffocating."

Our tears dropped simultaneously when he leaned his head down to kiss my lips. I could feel the electricity pass through my body into his as our tongues explored familiar territory. For a second I forgot how crazy everything was as I kissed my husband, the man I swore to love through sickness and health until death parted us. The man I bore children for, the love of my life.

As our kiss ended I knew that it was almost time to come back home to our house and live as a family again, but we had so much to talk about first. The closet was now wide open and skeletons were practically sprinting out of it and dancing on Broad Street. It was time for us to do some soul searching and come clean. Myself included.

For the next couple of hours we just sat and held each other, engrossed in our own thoughts. It wasn't until the sky turned burnt orange, indicating the end of another day, that I gathered the kids up so we could leave. They had a fit as we put them into the jeep. They did not want to leave their father. There were too many things left unsaid, too much hurt. James kissed the kids goodnight, then walked around to the driver's side where I was standing.

We embraced for what felt like an eternity, neither of us wanting to let go. We kissed one last time before I got into my jeep to leave. He leaned into the window to kiss me again. I pulled away, my tears making me see double for a second.

"Mommy, I miss Daddy. Will we be going back home soon?" Jalil asked as he and his sister yawned, trying to fight sleep. Their time in the yard had exhausted their little bodies.

"I miss Daddy too, baby. But don't worry, we'll be home soon enough."

That answer must have been good enough for both of them as we continued our ride back to my brother's house, but as I listened to the Quiet Storm on the radio, my thoughts wandered to a happier time in my life when everything felt like it was perfect. I wanted to be there again, but things had to be smoothed out first. It was going to take some time for us to completely heal and bounce back. We had to learn how to trust again, and that might be our biggest hump to get over.

I let the melody from the radio take me back to a time when I had no doubts. Now doubt was all over me like a second skin. I wanted to know so much, but in a way I didn't. Crazy thoughts ran rampant through my head all the way back to my temporary home. I wanted my life back, and was determined to get it, no matter what.

When I pulled into the driveway I could see my brother and his wife in the kitchen. I hated disturbing their household, feeling more like an intruder than a guest. Although my brother said he didn't mind the company, I felt like I was an added burden to their peaceful lives. They weren't used to kids, toys, and crayons everywhere.

By the time I turned the ignition off, my brother was outside helping me remove my sleeping babies from the backseat. I could see the concern in his eyes, and was thankful that he waited until the kids were in bed before he questioned me.

"So," he began with a sad look on his face, "how'd it go?"

I broke down in tears as I told him and his wife about my afternoon. It was so painful not being with my husband, and seeing him made it worse. I told him about the offer James made for us to talk tonight, and surprisingly my brother agreed. He gave me his blessing, assuring me that watching the kids wouldn't be a problem while I handled my business at home. He also warned me to keep my legs closed, reminding me that now wasn't the time to give in to lust. I kept his words and his blessing in my heart as I drove back to the city, back toward my husband, hoping to accomplish something positive.

James

Confessions

"*Everything that I've been doing is all bad. I gotta chick on the side with the crib and a ride. I been telling you so many lies. Ain't none good, it's all bad. I just wanna confess, it's been going on so long and I been doing you so wrong. And I want you to know that . . .*"

My heart had to be racing faster than the speed of light. Every time I saw a headlight flash through my window I jumped up, only to be disappointed to see the car pass by my driveway. My mind told me that Jazz wasn't coming back to talk, but my heart held on to the hope that she would. Every time my footsteps echoed around this empty house I missed the sounds and fulfillment of having my family there with me.

I remembered a time when we couldn't wait to fill our house with children. Every time I looked at Jasmine, whether she was awake or sleeping, I just wanted to be close to her because she was the love of my life. My father told me never to love anyone more than I loved myself, but when it came to my wife and kids, that was impossible. I would lay down my very soul to save theirs, and not having them as a part of my everyday life was killing me. Every time I stepped across the doorway I felt like all the oxygen had been sucked out of the room, leaving me to deal with my fears and skeletons on my own. My mistakes followed me around the house like a bad spirit.

OK, having an affair was a selfish act. Bringing Jazz into it made it worse, but that didn't mean I didn't love my wife and kids. It showed how stupid I was, and I was paying for it every time I stepped into my empty house.

Pacing back and forth in front of the couch was surely wearing out the carpet, but I couldn't rest. I wanted to hop in my car and follow her over, but I knew she wouldn't have liked that. I was trying to give her space so she could come to me willingly, but how much longer would I have to wait? It'd been like an hour and a half since she had left and I knew it didn't take that long to get to the north side. I wanted to call her brother's house, but I didn't want to seem too pushy. I felt like the walls were caving in on me as I tried to make sense of it all.

I got excited as I heard the sound of the doorbell and I figured it was Jazz.

I didn't want it to look like I was going through an ordeal. I wanted to look like I was chillin'. Taking a quick look around the room, I made sure the lamps were down low enough to set the scene. I pulled out the photo albums from our wedding day, her pregnancy, and pictures of the kids as they grew up, hoping they would aid in getting Jasmine to change her mind and come back. I had a bottle of apple cider chilled in a bucket with two glasses, not wanting any alcohol to cloud our vision and have us do something we would regret later. When I opened my door it was my neighbor reminding me to roll up my car windows before I turned in for the night.

A half hour later I found myself dozing off in front of the television. I was mad as hell that Jazz didn't show, but at the same time I didn't have a right to be mad. I got caught with my pants down, literally, and I couldn't really be all that upset that she didn't want to talk. Deciding to call it a night, I clicked the television off

The moment I turned off the television I heard the sound of a doorbell ringing, but I wasn't sure if that had been a sound that the televison made before I turned it off.

Hoping for the best, I quickly rushed to the door, but I paused before opening it because I didn't want to seem too anxious. Then the bell rang again, so I finally decided to open it up and let Jazz inside the house.

Unfortunately when I opened the door I got the absolute shock of my life. It wasn't Jazz who was standing at the door, it was the two strippers from the Cat House, Desire and Ina! The two of them were standing at my front door looking as strippered out as they could look, with the stilettos and all. They instantly got me aroused even though my heart had dropped to my feet because I knew Jasmine could be pulling up to the house at any moment.

"Hey, Papi!" Ina said in her thick, Puerto Rican accent. "We decided to stop by on our way to the club and see if you wanted us to hit you off before the night started." Ina continued while letting herself into the foyer of my house while simultaneously caressing my dick.

"Oh shit!" I said while I smirked a devilish laugh that was combined with a nervous smile.

Before I could say anything else, Desire had also entered into the foyer and proceeded to make her way into the living room. She looked as if she was preparing to take off her clothes so that we could do the damn thing. She made sure that she reminded me that it had been my idea to have her and Ina "surprise me" as she stated in a somewhat mocking tone.

"Yeah, yeah I know what I said. But listen for real for real both of y'all gots to go! Not now but right now! My wife is literally on her way here as we speak. I thought it was her at the door when the two of y'all rang the bell."

"See, Desire? I told you he was a fronting-ass nigga! We see them all the time in the club fronting like they got dough and shit but when it comes time to make it do what it do then they start frontin' and bitchin' up!" Ina stated.

"Nah, wait a minute. Fuck that! Yo' ass told us we could stop by here any night we wanted to to hit you off and you would hit us off with two hundred dollars apiece! Fuck that, I want my money! *Unannounced! Just show up and I got y'all!*" Desire stated as she mocked me by imitating what I had said to them one night. It had to have been the Hennessey that was talking for me when I had said that, but hey, I was in a jam and I had to think and act quick because if Jazz were to walk in on this then I could forget about it!

"Ok, ok. Look, I got y'all." I said as I reached into my pocket and pulled out a wad of money.

And just as I took out the money, sure enough I saw headlights outside.

"Ahh shit! Motherfucker!" I yelled as I had looked out the window and confirmed that the headlights were indeed Jasmine's.

"Listen! Just take this and split it. I'm sure it's more than enough and I don't have time to count it. That's my wife who just pulled up and if she finds the two of y'all in here she will kill all of us!"

"You know, I really don't need this bullshit!" Desire stated in her ghetto accent. "We got money to make. We don't have time to be playing around with you and your clown ass!"

"Desire, listen. Both of y'all please just do me this solid and hide in this closet right here next to the front door. I'll make sure I leave the front door open and when my wife comes in I'll walk to another room with her and when y'all don't hear us talking y'all can come out of the closet and walk out of the front door and bounce," I said in a rushed and panicked tone while pushing both Ina and Desire toward and into the foyer closet.

"I can't believe this nigga!" Desire stated as Ina sounded as if she were cursing me out in Spanish.

No sooner were the two of them crammed into the closet, than Jasmine was walking through the front door.

"Hey, James," she said as my heart raced a thousand beats per second.

I hesitated at first, but then held my arms open for a hug. She stepped into my arms without a second thought, and I closed my arms around her, hoping she didn't feel my thumping heartbeat. Although I was nervous as hell, it felt so good to have her body pressed against mine, her strawberry shampoo a familiar scent to me. She stepped back long enough to close the door and lock it.

We then sat down at opposite ends of the couch, leaving the middle cushion empty. Jasmine's back was to the foyer area where the two strippers were hiding. Neither one of us wanted to be the first to speak, but we both knew we had a lot of things to talk about. At this point I was ready to do whatever I had to do to have my family back. But as I looked and saw Ina and Desire tiptoeing in stilettos, making their way out of the closet and to the front door, I knew that if Jazz just slightly turned around that I could forget it as far as ever getting my family back.

"Well," Jasmine said as she looked everywhere but at me. *Thank God she didn't turn her head.* "I guess I should start by apologizing."

"For what?" I was confused. I was the one caught ass out on the table with her secretary and a woman I wasn't supposed to have any ties to outside of the threesome we had planned. All she ever did was try to be the woman I wanted her to be.

"For everything. The fact that you thought you had to step outside of our marriage to find satisfaction. If I was on point you wouldn't have had a reason to look anywhere else." I could see the tears welling up in her eyes, but what could I do? I could also see Ina and Desire safely making it out the front door and, man, was I ever relieved. I knew I could then focus on what Jasmine was actually saying.

"Jazz, listen, had I not pressured you into having the threesome in the first place, none of this would've happened. You only did it to make me happy, and it got out of hand. Monica was conniving anyway, and she wanted us to be at each other's throats. It's not your fault, Jazz."

"As true as that may be, James, I feel like we would have been cool if we had just talked. Tonight I'm going to tell you some things that may hurt you—things that you may never forgive me for—but I need to tell you what happened if only to clear my own heart so I can sleep at night."

"Baby, we don't have to get into all that now. We can take it one day at a time. I just need you and the kids back here with me. I can't live without you, Jazz." I was hoping my tactic was working because Lord knew I didn't want to tell her what really went down. She would be out of there for sure if she knew I wasn't straight with her about Monica and me from the beginning. And she would have really been out had I dry snitched on myself and told her about how I was wilding out with the strippers from the Cat House. And if there was one thing I knew, it was that there was no way in hell I was going to tell her about that.

We got comfortable—or as comfortable as was possible considering the situation—on the couch so we could talk further. The first thing she did was pick up our wedding album. I sat back and kept my mouth shut as she quietly flipped through the pages, some of the photos producing a slight giggle at the memory. She stared at some pictures a little longer than others. I let her take her time because I wanted things to be like they were then.

"So," she began after putting the album down, "let's get this done. I'll tell you everything you should know about the past year, and I want to know everything on your part. Answer the questions honestly no matter how hurtful, OK?"

"Cool." I was sweating already. What I had to say would cut deep, and I wasn't sure I was ready to reveal it. "Where do you want me to start?"

"The beginning. How did you really meet Monica?"

"I met her at a Bistro in Center City. She would always be there on my lunch break."

"So, the story about her being your friend's sister or whatever was a lie?" she asked as she got up and poured herself a glass of apple cider. The room seemed to get twenty degrees hotter in a matter of seconds. I didn't want to be questioned first, but somehow it was flipped on me, and I was stuck.

"Yes, I didn't want you to think she was just any ol' body off the street."

"So when did you actually start sleeping with her?"

"Maybe two weeks before we had the threesome," I lied with a straight face. It was more like two months before then, but I didn't want her to think she wasn't satisfying me for that long.

Yeah, I knew it was the time to lay all of the cards on the table so we could move on, but I just couldn't do it. Too much was at stake, and in keeping it honest, I really didn't think it was a matter of her not pleasing me. Jazz was a beast in the bedroom. I truly believed it was just one of those opportunities that maybe I shouldn't have taken advantage of.

"So, how did the threesome come about?" Jazz quizzed as she sipped from her cup. She didn't seem fazed by what I was telling her, but then again, who was to say she wasn't ready to cut me right then?

"Well, I was up front with her from the very beginning about being married. I guess she just kind of wore me down, and after I slept with her she kept pressuring me about bringing you in once I showed her a picture of you."

"I see. How many times did you sleep with her before we all got together?" Jazz asked with a straight face. She was too calm, and I wanted her to do something besides just sit there. I needed her to show some kind of emotion.

"Twice," I responded as I reached for a glass so I could drink something. She had only asked me a few questions, but I was already falling apart at the seams.

"So, after sleeping with her only twice she was able to convince you into convincing me?"

"Well, not exactly. I had been trying to get you to do it way before I met her, don't you remember? But it wasn't until she came along that I brought it back up, and I decided that if I had to share you with someone, why not Monica? You both looked beautiful together."

I was thinking I may have said too much because Jazz was looking like she was ready to blow. She was keeping her composure, but I could tell she was getting upset.

"How did Sheila become a part of the equation?" Jazz asked in a somewhat calm tone, but the look on her face and her body language showed she was ready to hurt somebody. I knew she said she wanted the truth, but I didn't think she wanted it as raw as I was giving it to her.

"Well, to be perfectly honest, I really don't know. After the threesome I saw Monica a couple of times when we happened to run into each other. Well, you know how persuasive Monica can be."

"Yeah, how 'bout that," she said as she picked up the other photo album and started flipping through it.

I could tell the conversation was getting to be too much

for her, but at that point I agreed we had to get it done so we could move forward. We hadn't even begun to scratch the surface, and there was still much more to work through.

"Well, is there anything you want to know about me?" Jazz asked.

"Just tell me what you think I should know."

As she flipped through the album she told me about the flowers Monica kept sending to her office, and how the woman Monica was talking about the day I saw her at the courthouse was her. She said she even contemplated leaving me to be with Monica on several occasions, but she didn't want to do that to the kids.

"James, you know I love you with all of my heart, and even though I thought about leaving, I knew it was pure lust that was pointing me in her direction, but you or our kids didn't deserve that."

She went into detail about how she went to Monica's house on nights when I thought she was working, and that Monica was determined to make her fall in love with her. She said she was hurt because even though we both were wrong, the position I got caught in was unforgettable, and she didn't really know what to do to get past it. I listened as my wife poured her heart out, and I felt like shit because I still wasn't keeping it totally real with her.

"So, is there anything else I should know, James? We need to get this out and over before it's too late," she said as she wiped tears from her cheeks. I wanted to hold her, but I knew there was no way to stop the hurt.

"Well, there is one thing," I said before clearing my throat. I was only telling her this because I didn't want her to find out from someone on the low. Yeah, I had left out a lot, but this would make or break our marriage, and I wasn't sure I could live with that.

"OK, what is it?" she asked as she moved to the end of the couch to stand up.

"Jazz," I began, placing my hand on her knee so she would remain seated, because if she stood up she would surely fall back down.

"James, just go ahead and say it, baby. Whatever it is, I can handle it."

"Well, baby . . . Monica's pregnant."

Monica

May, 1991

Monica,
   I've been liking you for a long time. Meet me behind the bleachers at three o'clock so we can make it happen . . . I think I love you.

                                                                Kevin

I got the note at nine in the morning when I went to get my algebra book out my locker for class. I must have read it at least fifty times during the course of the day, not believing what I read. Kevin was the captain of the school football team, and was fine as hell. He'd led the team to victory three years in a row, and all the college scouts were on him like crazy. I had been eyeballing him since I transferred to the Parkway Gamma High School, but who was I to approach anyone? That was my second year there, and he never looked my way or said anything to me until now. Yeah, he laughed at the jokes that I always managed to be the butt of, but he never said anything mean to me.

   Transferring to a new school was killing me. Between try-ing to make new friends, which didn't seem to be working out, keeping up in class, and keeping Uncle Darryl off me, I didn't think I was going to make it. I felt like the chick from *The Color Purple,* and Uncle Darryl was Mister. The only thing I was missing in this situation was the pretty sister to help me deal with the mess. She lucked up and got to stay with her people.

All I wanted to do was get my education so I could get the hell out of there. The people at school were not the least bit friendly, and I'd gotten into a fistfight or two because of it. Since I was considered the ugly duckling of the class, I was nowhere near popular.

Well, it was 2:53 p.m. By the time I put my books in the locker and walked across the field, Kevin should be there. Checking the mirror in my locker, I made sure my hair was in order as I put lip-gloss on my lips and slicked down my eyebrows. I took only the books I needed and stuffed the rest in my locker, rushing out the school so I could make it on time.

As I walked across the field, all kinds of thoughts rushed through my head. Maybe he was going to ask me to go with him to the junior prom. I had heard that he and Ashley broke up, so this would be right on time. Ashley was head cheerleader and a damn snob. She could jump the highest and had the longest pigtails. Every girl wanted to be her or be her friend. She treated me like shit, so I stayed far away from her and the members in her crew. I hadn't even discussed the prom with Uncle Darryl yet, but I would get around to it when he wasn't drunk. Whenever that was.

As I approached the bleachers I spotted Kevin sitting on his jacket smoking a joint. His eyelids were already at half-mast from the effects of the illegal drug he was puffing on. I took all of him in as I approached. His body was toned. His T-shirt stuck to his chest from the warmth of the afternoon, defining his muscles. By the time I sat next to him I was a wet mess and nervous as hell.

"You looking real cute in them jeans, girl." Kevin was rubbing his large hands up and down my legs, squeezing my thighs in the process. My nipples were hard on my flat, boy-like chest, making me sort of embarrassed that I was responding in that way.

"Thanks, Kevin. I'm glad you like them."

"I like you. I've been watching you for a while, waiting to kiss those pretty lips of yours. You have a sex appeal about you that I just can't explain, but I like it. I like it a lot," he said to me through kisses on my earlobe.

I was too naive to recognize game. All I knew was this didn't feel like what Uncle Darryl did to me on a regular basis. This felt real, like how it should be. I felt myself falling fast for him, and by the time his lips touched mine, I was in love.

Kevin Hall was six feet even, caramel-skinned, and handsome as hell. Curly hair showed signs of his ancestry—a mother who was Japanese and a father who was African-American and Cuban. His slanted, hazel eyes had all the ladies salivating over him in hopes of one day being the one to wear his team chain and football jacket. Out of all the girls in the school who were practically placing their panties in his hand, he had chosen to hang out with me on the one day he didn't have practice. I felt like I had just hit the lottery. I couldn't wait to see the expression on every girl's face in the school when I walked in with his jacket on, especially that damn Ashley. I would make it my business to see her.

"Look, it's getting kind of chilly. You wanna come to my house for a while? My parents won't be in until later tonight, so it's cool," Kevin said as he took one last drag off his joint before grinding it in the dirt with the heel of his boot. It was actually hot as hell under those metal bleachers, but if that was his way of inviting me to the crib, I would play along.

"Sure, that's cool, but I have to be home by five thirty or my uncle will have a fit."

"Not a problem. We'll be done by then."

I acted like I didn't hear his last comment as he helped me from the ground after dusting off the back of his jeans. We took the short way to the parking lot and hopped in his car so we could go to his house. His car was better than I'd expected. The engine was quiet on his 1990 Ford Tempo as we made our way down the street.

I melted in the leather seats as we listened to the Force MD's sing about tears falling like rain. He had me from then on. Everyone else our age was listening to Kwame, Kriss Kross, Black Sheep, and The Notorious B. I. G. It was nothing to ride by and hear NWA screaming out "Fuck The Police" and KRS-1 trying to educate his people.

Dollar parties were where we all hollered about being down with O. P. P. and none of us really knew what it was. Every girl wanted to be a "gangsta bitch" like the one Apache rapped about, and bamboo earrings made you an around-the-way girl. In a day when rap music was king, this man was listening to a sound that wasn't of his era. To me it made him look so much more mature, and it brought back memories of my mother and WDAS on the radio on Sunday nights.

He kept his eyes on the road, neither of us bothering to make small talk. I already knew what was going to happen, and I was trying to calm my nerves before we got there. My Uncle Darryl would have a fit if he knew I was with a boy and not at the library like I told him, but that was a chance I was willing to take. Out of all the girls he had, he chose me, and I was ready.

We pulled up to an enormous house not too far from the school. It was a single home with a well-groomed yard and a beautiful flowerbed. By the time I got my seatbelt off, he was already opening the door for me. I smiled as I exited the vehicle, grabbing my book bag.

The walk to his house felt like it was a mile long as we seemingly moved in slow motion all the way to his door. I heard nothing—no cars or anything else that I would normally hear on a busy afternoon. As I walked into his living room, I blocked out the outside world. It was like someone had hit the mute button, taking all of the sound from the planet. My heart was beating so fast I could have easily had a heart attack. Kevin appeared cool as he turned on the radio, and the song we were listening to in the car drifted from the speakers.

He took off his button-down shirt and sat down beside me. I damn near jumped out of my skin, because unlike outside, there was nowhere to run, no bleachers to hide behind, and no one to help me get out of the situation. It was just me, him, and my sweaty palms. I didn't want to seem immature in his eyes, so when he leaned over and began to unbutton my shirt, I held my breath until he was done.

He took my small breasts into his hands before releasing them from my bra. The entire time I was wondering why we didn't just go up to his room, but I was too shaken to speak. He pushed me back on his couch, and before I knew it my pants were undone and one leg was out. By then I was starting to panic, but I didn't want him to think I was scared.

I tried to steady my breathing as he pulled out his penis. He was almost as big as my uncle, and Lord knows it wouldn't fit inside me without ripping me in half. I moved to pull my pants back on and tell him I couldn't do it, but before I could sit up, four of his friends, guys I recognized from the football team, came out of his living room closet, each grabbing a hold of me and pinning me down to the couch. One held a pillow over my face so no one would hear me scream, causing me to turn my face to the side so that I could still breathe.

The more I struggled, the harder they gripped me. The room was dark and my face was behind the pillow, so I couldn't see who was doing what, and after a while I just gave up the struggle as they took turns having their way with me. Uncle Darryl had only gotten the head in, but these boys tore into me like a bullet, the burning sensation unbearable. I just closed my eyes and cried silently as I listened to the Force MD's sing on the radio. My tears fell like rain that day, and after they shoved me out the door once I put my clothes back on, I knew I would need a good, long cry as I made my way home.

Once I got home it went from bad to worse. Uncle Darryl was drunk as usual on the couch. One of his lady friends was over, but that really didn't matter. I'm sure if she didn't stay all night, he'd be in my room before the sun came up. Uncle Darryl wasn't a bad looking brother, considering the kind of man he was. Standing six feet three inches with a solid build, skin the color of vanilla wafers, and jade green eyes, women were practically throwing themselves at him. That's why I couldn't see what he wanted with little old me.

I spoke a weak hello as I made my way by them and went straight to the bathroom. Locking the door, I stood in the tub after a painful urination and washed between my legs, removing the blood and semen from my earlier ordeal. I was still bleeding, so I grabbed a clean pair of underwear and a maxi pad from the closet before changing into a pair of sweats and a T-shirt. I then went to clean the kitchen.

I was in a daze as I simultaneously washed dishes and started dinner. While everything was simmering on the stove, I swept and mopped the kitchen floor before starting my homework. It hurt like hell to sit down, so I folded one of my legs under me to ease the pressure of sitting flat on the chair.

My mind was still in a state of shock as I calculated math problems and held back my tears. I really thought Kevin liked me. Had I known it would come to this, I never would have gone to his house, but how could I know? How would I face him in school the next day? All of these thoughts raced through my head as I fed my uncle and his friend, and cleaned the kitchen for the night, unable to eat anything myself. Instead of turning on my little black and white television, I lay in the dark until I cried myself to sleep.

I finally fell into a comfortable sleep. Just as I was going to turn over, I felt my uncle slipping into the bed next to me. My body stiffened automatically, and I held my breath as he grabbed roughly at my breast, the smell of liquor evident on his breath.

"Uncle Darryl," I said through slightly parted lips as I held on to my pants. He was trying to pull them down and I was trying to keep them up. "Uncle Darryl, we can't do this. My period is on."

"Girl, since when did that matter? You know my motto, don't chu girl? Don't chu?" he asked as he continued to pull on my pants and tears ran down the sides of my face.

"Yes, Uncle Darryl," I said between sobs. "I know the motto."

"Then what is it?" he replied after he finally got my pants down and his Johnson out. "Say it, bitch! What is it?"

"Walk through mud . . . fuck through blood," I said as he ripped my pants the rest of the way off and entered me fully for the first of many times.

"And don't chu ever forget it!"

For the next hour he forced himself inside me, my stiffness not a concern of his in the least. For what seemed like the hundredth time that night, I cried silent tears as he took advantage of me over and over again. When he finally left, I didn't bother to move as I watched his silhouette through the light in the door. He didn't even bother to put it back in as he rumbled through his pockets and threw something on the floor.

It wasn't until morning that I discovered the two crumpled twenty-dollar bills and a Trojan condom wrapper. I picked the money up before I went to take a shower, only doing so after I made sure the coast was clear and Uncle Darryl had left for work. When I came back into the room I put that money with the rest of the money I got from him every time he did what he did to me.

In the back of my closet I had an old mayonnaise jar that I

used to hide the money. Tears streamed down my face as I unfolded the six hundred dollars I already had there, adding the forty dollars to the bounty. One day I would have enough to move out, and hopefully that day would come soon.

When I got to school the next day, it felt like all eyes were on me. As I walked through the hallways in a daze, it seemed like everyone stopped what they were doing to look at me. I was still numb from the events of the previous day, so by the time I got to my locker I was unaware of the small crowd forming behind me.

After three tries I finally got the combination to my locker to work. When I opened it up piles of condoms fell out and landed at my feet. All I could do was stare as the crowd behind me burst into laughter. I didn't even know how the condoms got in there, and I made no effort to pick them up as I took out the books I needed, causing more to fall from my locker and onto the floor. Closing the locker, I turned to squeeze through the crowd only to find myself face to face with Ashley.

"Figured you may need those since you like the group thing," Ashley said, getting another round of laughter from the crowd. She had on Kevin's jacket and chain. That was another slap in the face.

Embarrassed, I pushed through the crowd before they could see my tears drop. I walked as fast as I could down the hallway, stopping to pick up the books that kept falling from my arms along the way, the crowd taunting me in the background.

"There's some plastic wrap here, too. Just in case you decide you wanna be a blow fish again," Ashley called out behind me.

I kept up the pace as I made my way to the principal's office. Taking a seat on the bench, I put my head down so I could catch my breath. It was obvious that Kevin and his

goons came back and told the entire school that I willingly
had sex with them yesterday. By the time the office aide noticed me sitting there, I was a mess. She told the principal I
was out there, and walked me into her office so we could
talk. I could hear "Tears" playing from the small radio on the
principal's desk as she got up to close the door behind the
secretary. I put my head on the desk and cried, wondering to
myself how my life had ended up this way.

*As the sun sets and the night comes around I can feel my
emotions coming down. But now I pull the covers off my bed
saying to myself, "tonight I'll forget . . ."*

Jasmine

Full Of Surprises

"So, you're telling me that Monica is having your baby?" I said to James with so much venom dripping from my voice it could have burned a hole in the floor. I know he didn't just tell me some bullshit like that. Honestly, I wasn't even sure why I was so surprised, because when they were propped up on my damn table there surely wasn't any protection popping off. I damn sure don't remember seeing any condom wrappers on the floor that day, so why would they have used one any other time?

"I'm telling you that's what she told me, but I haven't spoken to her since then, so I'm not sure how true it is."

"And if she is, James, what are you going to do?"

At that point I felt like my world was crumbling around me. I swear, every time I thought I could pick up the pieces and put everything back together, another issue came around, messing it all up again. It was like I had a black cloud hanging over my head. Haters were always trying to knock a bitch back.

The fact that James was so cool about the situation was pissing me the hell off. If—and I stress the word "if"—

Monica was indeed pregnant, she was not giving that baby up. She'd keep it just to make me miserable, and I'd be damned if I wanted that constant reminder in my face every day. James and I had our owns kids to raise, and not that we were hurting for cash, but her having James's baby would be another mouth to feed, even if it was only part time. Call it cruel, but I didn't want that baby anywhere near me and my kids. It was as simple as that.

Looking over at James, I wanted to knock that stupid ass look off his face. I was trying so hard not to place all the blame on him, but if he hadn't pressured me into that threesome shit, none of this would be happening. I wanted to jump on his neck and choke the shit out of him, but on the flip side I was disappointed in myself for letting it go that far. I honestly was trying to please my husband in the beginning, but then it got way out of hand. I had no business being over at that woman's house either, and I knew it.

Starting to feel lightheaded and a tad on the nauseous side, I took a seat on the arm of the couch so I could gather my thoughts and get my head on straight before I went back to my brother's house. More than ever I was hoping my black clouds did have a silver lining. I had to put my life back together before it was too late.

"James, we'll talk about this some more, but not today. Right now I don't have the energy," I said to him as I moved to make my way toward the door. I felt like I was moving in slow motion as the room began to spin violently around me. I felt like I was watching myself from the sidelines. The last thing I remember before the room went black was reaching for my coat and trying to remember where I had placed my car keys.

When I came to, my head was pounding. I finally focused in on James after adjusting my eyes to the light. He was looking down at me with a worried expression on his face. He was sweating profusely, and he appeared to have the shakes.

I wanted to lift my head from the pillow, but doing so made my head pound harder. I looked around the room and tried to figure out where I was. I didn't remember James telling me he had painted our guest room. Still feeling delirious, I was trying to think if the bed had railings on it before today.

"Jazz, how are you feeling, baby? Are you thirsty?"

"No, I'm fine. My head just hurts. Where's my coat?"

"Jazz, you can't leave until the doctor is finished evaluating you."

"What?" For the first time I realized that I was not in the comfort of my own home, but I was in a hospital room instead.

"Yeah, you passed out at the house and bumped your head on the edge of the end table. We've been here for a couple of hours. I was scared I lost you."

"James, I . . ."

"Baby, just rest. The doctor should be back any minute."

Taking the cup of ice from James, I sat back on the bed, trying to gather my thoughts. I must be really stressed out because I'd never passed out before. This shit with James was working my last nerve. My thoughts flip flopped from wanting things to work, to wanting it all to be over. Just as I was dozing off again, the doctor walked in.

"Mrs. Cinque, I'm glad to see you're awake. How's your head feeling?" The doctor quizzed as he touched the bottoms of my feet to see if I was responsive before moving up to listen to my heartbeat.

"My head is pounding something awful, but I'll survive."

"That's good to hear, although you do have a nasty bump on your head. Do you mind if I ask you a few personal questions?"

"No, not at all. What do you need to know?" I responded as my heart began to pound wildly in my chest. I hope he's not about to tell me I have a deadly disease. I have enough shit going on in my life.

"Have you been under a lot of stress lately? When you came in your blood pressure was abnormally high."

"Well, things have been a little hectic lately, but nothing outside of the norm," I lied after taking a quick peek at James. I wish I could have told the doctor what the real deal was, but that was a little too much information, and I didn't need him in my business.

"When was your last menstrual period? Has it been coming on a consistent basis?"

I couldn't answer right away because it'd been at least two months since I'd seen it. I didn't really pay it that much attention, contributing its absence to all of the stress I'd been under lately, but now I wasn't too sure.

"It was maybe two months ago. I didn't have one last month, and it's a little late this month, but it'll come. I've just been stressed."

"Well, Mrs. Cinque, we took some blood when you first arrived and the tests show that you're pregnant. We're going to do an ultrasound to find out how far along you are. I'll have the nurse . . ."

I didn't hear anything the doctor said after that. Did he just tell me I was pregnant? I was stuck on what I should do next. Now was not the time to be having another baby. James and I had too much to work out, and I still hadn't found out if Monica was having James's kid. My life was pretty much spiraling out of control, and I had no clue as to what I should do to fix it.

"So I'll send the nurse right in and we'll see what's what, OK?"

I nodded, still in shock at what the doctor told me. When he left the room, James came over, stood on the side of the bed, and took hold of my hand. I was starting to feel sick all over again just thinking about what we were facing.

"James, I can't have this baby," I stated matter-of-factly, not caring what he thought. I refused to bring another child into the drama that was going, and it didn't look like things would be getting better any time soon.

"What do you mean, you can't have the baby? Why not? I hope this has nothing to do with Monica," James practically screamed, nearing hysteria. For a few quick seconds I thought he was going to snatch me up.

"We already have issues we need to work through, and a baby would just complicate things."

"Things aren't that complicated, Jazz. How can you make that kind of decision for both of us?"

"Both of us? Did you think about both of us when . . ." before I could finish, the nurse walked in. James and I were steaming, but we managed to hold our tongues.

I was almost in tears as the nurse smeared a cool gel over my belly so she could perform the ultrasound. Flashbacks of when I was carrying my twins caused tears to spill over my eyelashes and run down the sides of my face. I wasn't ready for this. Not under these circumstances.

When I heard the baby's heart beat my tears flowed even more. As the nurse moved the monitor around on my belly I could see a figure the size of a tennis ball on the screen. I thought to myself about the possibility of having this baby, and how it would affect our lives. Was having this baby a good idea?

As I lay on the bed with my eyes closed, I could hear two heartbeats getting louder. Instantly I took it as my own and the baby's, but how could that be? When I opened my eyes to look at the monitor there were now two figures on the screen. I didn't want to believe my eyes. Could I be having . . .

"Well, Mrs. Cinque, it looks as if you're carrying twins," the nurse said happily. All I could do was stare at the screen and hope I was seeing double. As if one baby wasn't stressful enough, the size of my family had just doubled in a matter of minutes.

"Did you say twins?" James asked with a cheerful voice. He

knew I would have a hard time getting rid of one, so two was definitely out of the question. I'd never be able to do it.

"Yes, you guys are having twins. We'll be keeping you overnight for observation, Mrs. Cinque, just to make sure you're OK and no harm was done to the fetuses from your fall. The wait shouldn't be that long. I'm going to check for room availability now. The doctor will be in to talk to you shortly."

I was quiet as the nurse removed the gel from my stomach before readjusting my bed. On the way out she congratulated me and James on our new additions before closing the door to give us some privacy.

A million thoughts raced through my head as I turned to think of a way out of this. In my heart I knew there was only one, but I'd never do it. How could I? My babies deserved a chance at life . . . no matter how fucked up it may be.

James came and stood quietly by my side, and I continued to stare at the wall. What if Monica was carrying twins, too? That would be six mouths to feed! We had money, but damn. That would put a hurting on anyone's pocket. The thing was, Monica probably didn't even want the baby. Then again, who was I to say? If she didn't want a baby, she wouldn't have tried so hard to get pregnant.

I lay there not really focusing on anything, but thinking many things at once. James laid his head on my stomach. I refrained from touching him because I wasn't ready to forgive him. I still wanted to be mad at him. Hell, I needed to be mad because otherwise I'd give in too easily.

"Jasmine, I can't apologize enough for everything I put you through. I was wrong, and I admit it, but please don't take my babies away from me. We can make it work. I'm sure we can make it work," James said as tears ran from his eyes and onto my belly. I could feel my heart tug on my emotions, but I couldn't give in just yet.

"James, we'll talk about it later."

He didn't respond. He just pulled his chair up next to the bed and kept his head on my stomach until the doctor told us the room was ready. When we got upstairs and were settled, the doctor gave me a prescription for pre-natal vitamins and iron pills. He gave me instructions to make an appointment with my gynecologist within the next couple of days just to make sure everything was going well. After wishing us a successful pregnancy, he went on to treat the many patients in the emergency room.

James put his head back on my stomach, and this time I rubbed the back of his head, thinking of my next move. They had yet to tell me how far along I was.

Reaching over, I decided to call my brother before he started worrying. I should have been home hours ago. After dialing the number, the phone rang three times before he answered it.

"Hello, Robinson residence," my brother Dave sang into the phone, sounding like he was in a really good mood. His wife, Sarayah, must have broken him off a little something. Despite the obvious turmoil my heart was in, I still giggled a little in response to my big brother's happiness.

"Hey, it's me," I spoke into the receiver, trying to hide my sadness. I didn't want to alarm him.

"Hey, Sugar Pop. How'd everything go?" he asked, calling me by my childhood nickname. My family called me that because I wanted to eat Honey Smacks cereal for breakfast, lunch, and dinner every day. Sugar Pop was the name of the cartoon frog on the box.

"Not as good as expected, but I'll live."

"Well, when it comes to matters of the heart, you have to take it one day at a time."

"I know," I replied, hesitant to begin my next sentence. "I called to let you know I'm in the hospital, and they're keeping me overnight."

"You're where? In the hospital? For what? Did that nigga put his hands on you?" he shot off.

"No, he didn't put his hands on me, silly. You know he wouldn't do that."

"So, how did you end up in the hospital, Jazz?"

"I passed out at the house and woke up in the emergency room. James said I accidentally hit my head on the side of the table."

"Damn, girl, you all right? Want me to come get you?"

"No, I'm OK. James is still here."

"Good. That's good to hear. So what did they say? Stress?"

"I'm pregnant," I blurted out before I lost the nerve. I felt funny saying the words out loud, and my body cringed at the thought.

"Say word. Are you serious?" he asked, full of excitement. I wish I could've mustered up half his enthusiasm.

"With twins."

"With . . . " the phone got silent for about ten seconds and I wasn't sure if he hung up or passed out.

"You there?" I heard rustling in the background and before I knew it, Sarayah was talking into the phone.

"Jazz, congrats! Now I know why you were sleeping all the time. Girl, you were getting a little thick," she yelled into the phone, just as excited as my brother. "Honey, I can't wait until we have ours."

"So, I take it the twins didn't drive you crazy?"

"Oh, no. We had a ball when they woke up. Those little angels are back to sleep now."

"Angels? My kids?" I said as we shared a laugh over the phone. It felt good to be happy about something finally, even if only for a moment.

"Well, Jazz, I do hope you feel better, and I'll see you when you get home, OK?"

"OK, and tell your crazy husband I'll talk to him later."

After hanging up the phone, I lay back and stared at the ceiling. Telling my brother I was pregnant was my way of not doing anything stupid, like going through with the abortion. I cracked myself up talking like I would really do it, but right then I was stressed the hell out.

"Jasmine, I'm sorry I hurt you," James said, turning his head around so he could have his head on my stomach and look at me.

"James, we'll talk about this later."

"But baby, I just wanted to . . ."

"James, we'll talk later."

"OK, later is fine."

"OK."

I finally turned the television on, not really paying attention to the program that was playing. I had to get in contact with Monica sooner rather than later. We had a lot of things that needed to be discussed.

As I lay there I remember just wanting to scream to no end because life wasn't supposed to be like this. I lay there in a daze staring at the television, thinking to myself how I had a lot to discuss with Monica, but in reality who was I fooling? See, Monica was a major part of my problems, but I also knew that the twins from the gym, Donnie and Rahmel had ran all up in me and nutted up in me not too long ago and I didn't want to think it, but in my heart of hearts I knew that the twins that I had just found out that I was carrying weren't James's babies. Those babies inside of me had to be fathered by the twins from the gym! A woman knows who the father of her kids are; it's sort of like a spiritual, instinctual thing. I couldn't deny what I was feeling, and inside I knew that those kids couldn't be James'.

Lord, I can't take this drama! I remember thinking to myself. But no matter what, I knew that I could never let James onto the little secret I had which now had blossomed into a major secret being held inside my womb.

Carlos

It's A Small World: Today's News

News about Rico's suicide had been in the paper every day for the last three months. I was already stressing over the case I had. Yeah, they was trying to get me, but I kept my business as clean as possible so they'd need to try a little harder. Hell, Rico didn't even get props like that when he was walking the streets. Every time I turned on the television or picked up the *Daily News*, I saw his face plastered all over it, like his spirit wouldn't let me have any peace.

Shit, he had it coming! Every hustler in this game knew you couldn't get out. You either disappeared or died trying. Rico knew it was just a matter of time before he was slayed. He had enemies from here to the end of the earth, so his days had been numbered for years. Rico was a lot of things, but suicidal? Naw . . . he would never die a sucker's death. That dude was a soldier. He expired before my connect had a chance to get at him. I knew his supplier, but damn if I knew if he was willing to do business.

Bitches were practically throwing their panties in his casket at the funeral, and that Monica bitch didn't even have

the decency to show up. She could have at least faked it 'til
the very end. Damn! That bitch had no class, and it made
her look suspect.

I just felt bad for Shaneka . . . sort of. She was ride or die
for Rico, and he just tossed her to the birds like she never
meant shit to him. That woman was a ticking time bomb,
and I was just laying low, waiting for her to explode. They
had broken up and got back together plenty of times, but
that last time was murder. He scooped Monica's ass up quick
as shit, and it was like a slap in the face to Shaneka. All I
could say was when Monica got dealt with, it wasn't gonna be
nothing pretty about it. Monica played that "Oh, I'm crazy"
shit, but Shaneka was certified. That girl got papers and was
not to be fucked with.

I wasn't banking on Monica getting off as easy as she did.
It seemed like she woulda taken the fall with Rico, but it did-
n't turn out like that. It was almost like she was fucking the
judge or something.

I'd be seeing Monica about some shit real soon. Rico had
gravy beyond your wildest imagination, and I knew she
walked away laced. When his peeps came to clean out his
apartment that thing was practically empty. I knew my man
was living lavish, but you could never tell by how his place
looked when his peeps rolled through. It was like he never
even lived there. Clothes, shoes, jewels . . . everything was
gone, like my man never existed. Like maybe he was a fig-
ment of your imagination. He never introduced Monica to
his family, so no one knew who to look for, but I had my eye
on her ass from the gate. Snakes recognize other snakes, and
I knew her ass was kin. I was just mad she got to him before I
could.

One day right after Rico had died I was on the block, trying to push this powder while I still could. The Feds were trying to sweep the whole neighborhood on some bullshit, and

I had things to do. I couldn't be sitting up in nobody's penitentiary doing time. Yeah, I was a hustler but, I wasn't made for that shit. Give that to the real gangsters. Yeah, I be out here bustin' them guns when necessary, but when it came to doing time, I was a wankster all damn day. You wouldn't have my ass scared to pick up the soap.

I was about to head back because the same cop car done circled the block three times. I didn't know who they were looking for, but if it was me, that day wouldn't be the day. On the way back to the crib I decided to stop and get me a sandwich and a Pepsi when my cell phone rang. Looking down at the caller ID, I decided to ignore the call. Blocked numbers didn't get answered, and whoever was blowing my hip up should've known that. My phone rang four more times before I got to the crib, and whoever it was never left a message. Oh well.

I was sitting around trying to put a plan together. I'd been with Rico to visit his supplier plenty of times, but you just couldn't be approaching people like that, unless, of course, you had a death wish or something. I knew someone knew who did Rico, because personally I wasn't convinced he did it himself. Gangsters worldwide had been trying to get at him for the longest, and I just needed to find out what crew got him done so I could make my next move.

Taking a peek at my phone, I had twenty-seven missed calls from an anonymous caller, and it was working my nerves. Hell, it could be some chick I met recently or my worst nightmare on the other end. Either way, I wasn't interested. I was curious though, so I decided if the phone rang again, I might answer it.

Around seven thirty my anonymous caller buzzed my phone again, interrupting my favorite show, *Jeopardy*. I was pissed because the caller made me miss a question. Yeah, I was street, but I was not a complete idiot, you dig? A brother had to keep up with what was going on in the world. Anyway, already annoyed, I picked up the phone, my agitation clearly evident in the tone of my voice.

"State ya purpose, quick!" I growled into the phone. I didn't make it a habit of answering calls when I didn't know who was on the other end. I was knee deep in illegal shit, and the last thing I needed was the jakes on my ass. Only a handful of niggas knew the math, so for someone to call me with a blocked number spelled trouble.

"Carlos, it's me, Shaneka," the soft, feminine voice responded from the other end of the phone line. She sounded like she was crying, but that was none of my concern. The only nigga that gave a damn was dead now, so what did she want me to do? Instead of responding to her obvious cry for attention, I straight blacked on her like she was one of my many enemies.

"What I tell you about calling out my government, and why in hell are you calling me from a blocked number? You know I don't play those games."

"Well, C-Dogg, I had some valuable information for you, but since you want to act like a damn nut—" she spoke into the phone sarcastically. I could almost see the look on her face, probably a smirk with her eyebrows raised.

"Listen, speak ya piece, OK? If you got info, spill it. If not, get off my dime," I barked into the phone, cutting her off.

The part that killed me the most was that she acted like she was all bent out of shape over Rico's passing, but the entire time they were together I was tapping her ass to no end. Hell, the day he got busted I had just finished tearing her guts up before I went over there. She would come and blow me early in the morning, then later that day I'd see her tongue kissing Rico like my soldiers weren't just tickling her tonsils a few hours before. Snakes! Kin always recognized kin.

"Damn, since when has it been like that between us? You act like I never done you right."

"Shaneka, please tell me what I need to know, ma." I counted to ten to bring my blood pressure down. I had to refrain from banging on her ass because I swear we'd be arguing like we were a fuckin' couple. This girl was trying my last nerve early in the game.

"If you insist," she responded, sounding like she had shit in check. I decided to let her have that small victory for now. "Well, remember when I told you I thought I saw Monica before?" she asked, knowing damn well we'd already had that conversation.

"Yeah, I remember, why?"

"Well, peep this shit . . ."

Shaneka broke everything down from when she met Monica a while back up at the prison. The same guard Shaneka told me she was having problems with was giving Monica heat. As payback they did a number on the guard's car by slashing all four tires and putting a mixture of sugar, popcorn kernels, and Snickers candy bars in her gas tank. So even if the guard got new tires, by the time she started the engine, and that mixture started circulating, the car would be no good.

Come to find out Shaneka and Monica were visiting the same person. The men are housed about a mile down the road, but the visiting room is shared by both sexes to make it easier to keep track of the prisoners during visiting hours since none of the guards wanted to do any real work anyway.

Shaneka had been seeing a woman named Tanya for over a year and a half before Monica started to visit Tanya. Shaneka was rotating between seeing her brother one week and Tanya the next. Monica always visited Tanya on the week Shaneka wasn't seeing her, but Shaneka remembered what Tanya said about Monica's involvement with Tanya ending up on lockdown. It just didn't click in Shaneka's mind who Monica was until after Monica gave her a business card.

Shaneka met Tanya on a day she and her mom were visiting with her brother, and they had been cool ever since. She told Tanya that she would help her when she got out, and they became fast friends, and later on lovers. Rico never knew what was going on. Shaneka was practically running circles around him.

Her hate came about for Monica when they broke up and she found out Rico saw Monica that same day. Never mind that Monica knew nothing about Rico and Shaneka. Her vendetta was definitely personal on getting Monica back.

"So, what does all of this have to do with me?" I asked after missing several questions on *Jeopardy* while trying to pay attention to what Shaneka was saying.

"I'm getting to that now," she sighed, getting a little attitude because I had cut her off again.

She went on to talk about all the similarities between them, and how they knew a lot of the same people with both of them being photographers and artists. I think I heard her say something about a pink bitch, but I wasn't sure. She rambled on for about another ten minutes before I had to cut her off again. The information she was giving me I already knew, or didn't give a damn about, so what was the purpose of the call?

"Shaneka, please get to the point, damn!"

"OK, OK. Damn . . . so angry," she replied, afterward sucking her teeth. I didn't give a damn.

"Well, how about I saw her at the doctor's office this morning and you are not going to believe me when I tell you this!"

"Tell me what, Shaneka?"

"How 'bout that bitch is pregnant."

"And?" I said more than asked, confused as to why I should give a damn. Hell, it wasn't my seed.

"And? Nigga, I think it may be Rico's," she said, bursting into tears again. Now I knew why she was so upset.

"And you care because?"

"I care because that bitch stole my man, had him killed, and now she's having his baby."

"How you know she had Rico killed?" I asked, curious as to where she got her information. I thought maybe she knew something I didn't.

"I don't, but I think she did. Anyway, she's pregnant by my man. That's what's important."

"So what you gonna do?"

"Get her ass back! What the hell you mean what I'm gonna do?"

"I meant how, Shaneka, damn!"

"I'll get back to you on that by the end of the day, but I do have a tad bit of info that may work to your advantage."

"Word? What's that?" I asked, now bored with the conversation. I had my own neck to protect. Her shit was on solo this time.

"You know that cute little young girl that you be fuckin' all crazy over in Tasker projects? The one you got twisted on that coke?"

"Yeah," I said, now listening more to what she had to say.

"Well, if you're looking for a way to get at Monica, that's it. That pretty little young thing you got turned out is Monica's little sister."

Before I could say anything else, she hung up the phone, and I had a million questions I wanted to ask her. One thing I could honestly say about Shaneka was this: she may have been a little on the annoying side, but when she had some info she was usually on point—99.9 percent like a paternity test. I must say that shit she had just dropped on me was heavy, and I had to take a step back before I made my next move.

It's funny how small the world is, because I would have never in a million years connected Yoyo with Monica. Yolanda was a cutie for sure. Small waist, bubble butt, perfect breasts with kissable nipples, and the same heart-shaped mouth like her older sister. They were both dimes, the only difference being their last names. Maybe that's why I hadn't put two and two together.

As fly as Yoyo was, and as good as that pussy felt while she was riding me, she had one hell of a damn habit. My girl got her snort on, and was serious with it. Now, don't get me wrong, she didn't look like your average Joe Crackhead, but that girl would snort all day if the blow was available. And talk about wild sex! Man, that shit must run in the family because this chick was a beast.

One night I slid through for my waxing and she answered the door ass naked holding a silk scarf in one hand, and two pair of handcuffs in the other. My man came to life instantly, causing my pants to tent majorly in the front. She didn't say anything to me. She just dropped the handcuffs and scarf on the floor, and walked toward her bedroom in the back of the apartment.

Now, I ain't gonna lie, I was stuck on dysfunctional for a hot second. I knew she liked being creative, but sometimes she didn't give me a clue. I just had to walk in there and do my own thing. So now my mind was racing a mile a minute as I bent over to pick up the items from the floor before locking the door. She had a fly little apartment and she kept it neat, so I made sure to hang my coat up before going into the bedroom.

When I walked in, Yoyo was on the bed lying on her side with one leg up to her chest working a dildo from the back. Her other hand helped keep her nipples in her mouth as soft moans escaped her lips. I damn near exploded watching her in that somewhat compromising position. Shedding my clothes quickly, I joined her on the bed.

First turning her on her back, I tied the scarf she gave me around her eyes so she couldn't see what I was doing to her. Grabbing another scarf from the nightstand, I tied her hands tightly to the headboard so she couldn't move. I had to take a second and slow down before it was over, and it hadn't even started yet. Looking at her body stretched out on the bed, and my name tattooed across her pelvis where hair should be, almost had me wanting to wife her . . . almost.

Taking both pairs of handcuffs, after placing the keys in her hand, I first attached them to my wrist then to her ankles so she couldn't move. Yolanda was practically double jointed so I knew if I stretched her any which way she'd be able to conform. Normally, head was out of the question and never part of the equation, but that night I decided to show her what it was really hittin' for.

Since my hands were connected to her ankles I pushed her legs up and out as far as they could go comfortably. I would suck on her clit softly, making it real wet, then I'd blow on it until it got cold, warming it with my mouth and cooling it off repeatedly. It was interesting to sit back and watch as her cream began to rise to the top and gather at her opening.

I took the tip of my tongue and traced the edge of her tunnel in a complete circle before I stuck my tongue inside her, tasting her sweet, yet tangy nectar. I tugged on her clit softly with my teeth, leaning back so I could watch her juice spill over the sides and run down, my tongue catching it at her asshole.

Yolanda was practically begging me to slide up in her, but I wasn't ready yet. Pushing myself up on my knees I held on to her feet while I used my hips to rub the head of my man back and forth across her already sensitive clit. I would push just the head in, then pull it out and rub it across her clit again. Each time I went in, I pushed a little deeper until I was all the way inside her. I was killing the pussy with long, slow strokes, sometimes pulling out until just the tip of my dick was pressed against her, her walls gripping me like a Hoover trying to suck me back in.

Leaning in, I took her nipples into my mouth one at a

time, since I couldn't push them both together with my hands. I grinded my hips into hers, causing another series of explosions.

"Now, I'm gonna untie you, but I'm not taking the handcuffs off. You ready to ride?"

Instead of answering, she threw her legs back farther so I could untie the scarves from her eyes and wrist. Once she was untied, I grabbed her by her ankles and she held onto my neck as I maneuvered our bodies so she could be on top. My girl did the damn thing to me, un-cuffing me so I could hold on to her waist. Yolanda rode me until I was bone dry. Afterward she retrieved the eight ball from my coat pocket. She worked for that nose candy, so I just sat back and gathered my thoughts while she did her thing.

Thinking back, that was the last time I was over there, and from the imprint in my sweat pants, it was time to pay her ass another visit. While she worked me over I could see what info she would give me about her sister. They didn't appear to be close, and Yolanda was always out for self, so I was sure she could tell me something good. Making the call, she was all too happy to hear from me. We made plans to meet up before the week was out, and she made sure I knew what to bring with me.

Shortly after, just as I was reaching into my pants for a quick release, my cell phone buzzed indicating an incoming call. This time, Shaneka's number flashed across the screen. Peeping the time, I saw that it was ten o'clock at night. Damn, where did the time go?

"Yeah," I answered, feigning sleep. Unless she had more info, I wasn't in the mood to talk.

"Carlos . . . I mean C-Dogg, I need you to drop a package off at FedEx for me in the morning."

"On the real, Shaneka, I really don't want no part of whatever you tryna pull off. I got my own shit to deal with."

"Come on, C. You know I can't go into FedEx since I got into that fight with the manager."

"That's not my problem. Ain't nobody tell you to be in there on that hood shit. Go to another one."

"Come on! It ain't like you delivering a damn bomb. It's a gift for Monica."

"Oh word? What is it?" I asked, curious as to how she was planning to get Monica back.

"It's nothing really. Just a little something to let her know I got my eye on her. Can you please drop it off for me, please?"

"All right, already. Bring the shit by tonight, and I'll drop it off in the morning."

"I'm on my way."

After hanging up the phone, I hopped in the shower. Since she was coming over, I thought I might as well get fucked nice. That should hold me until Saturday.

Monica

One Dawn, More to Go—1991

I ended up telling the principal only half the story because I didn't want to have to explain the previous day's events to my uncle. I used the excuse that I wasn't feeling well so I could leave early. I walked home so I could take time to think, and I became a new person with each step. I was tired of Uncle Darryl having his way, and having to deal with the ridicule from the students in school. I was determined it all would end that day. In my mind I hatched a plan that would get my revenge on every person who ever did me wrong—especially those snotty-ass cheerleaders and that damn Ashley.

When I got home I ran up to my room and dropped my book bag in the corner. Standing in the mirror I took a look at my hair, deciding to loosen the ponytails. I went to my stash, took out three hundred dollars, and left the house, moving quickly toward the strip so I could get everything I needed and be home before my uncle got in.

Stopping at the hair store first, I picked up a mild relaxer, a can of Isoplus oil sheen, electric flatirons, and a satin cap to sleep in. Once I paid for my items I walked three doors down to "The Style Shop," a clothing store that sold fashionable items at cheap prices. I tried on outfit after outfit and finally settled on five pairs of jeans with matching shirts, shoes, and purses.

Clasping the bags tightly to my chest, I raced back home with three hours to spare. Hiding my new clothes in the back of the closet behind the boring clothes Uncle Darryl bought for me, I sat down to read the directions on the Dark & Lovely relaxer kit. I didn't want to risk my hair falling out from the procedure. Things were hard enough to deal with already without adding fuel to the fire. Following the directions, I worked the chemical into my hair until it was straight, and shampooed my hair three times to ensure all of the cream was removed.

After rinsing the conditioner and blowing my hair dry, I plugged in my brand new flatirons so they would be nice and hot when I was done cleaning up the mess I made in the bathroom. Taking a pair of scissors from the kitchen drawer, I trimmed my ends, afterward taking small sections of my hair and binding them into a soft, bouncy wrap.

Satisfied with my look, I then wrapped my hair into a beehive like I had seen my mother do to her hair many times, and tied a bandana tightly around it so it would be perfect in the morning. Getting rid of the evidence, I proceeded to clean the house and prepare dinner before my uncle arrived home. As I cleaned, I decided I would use a little more of the money I'd stashed to buy more clothes so I could keep up appearances.

I took the sharpest knife from the kitchen drawer, ran upstairs, and placed it under my pillow after I had made my bed. I didn't think I could kill my uncle, but if he came in my room again, he would get it. I would be buying a lock for my door tomorrow, whether he liked it or not. After finishing my homework, I ate dinner, cleaned up my mess, and took a bath. I put lotion on my skin so it wouldn't be dry, then got into bed to get some sleep.

My uncle came into the house around eight that night with one of his many girl toys. I woke up when I heard him come in, and I fed him and his company dinner, then cleaned the kitchen for the night. As I was walking by, he reached out and smacked me on my ass. I turned to say something, but before I got a word in, his lady friend was cursing him out.

"Darryl, you ain't got no business touching that girl like that. Keep ya hands to ya self!"

"Bitch, mind ya business! This here is family business."

"Oh, I know you ain't just call me a bitch? Nigga, I'll . . ."

While they argued back and forth I made my way upstairs. I felt relief for a second because I never had anyone take up for me. Everybody always acted like they didn't know what was going on. At the same time, I wished she would've kept her mouth shut because I'd have to pay for it later.

Once I was upstairs, I didn't bother to turn the television on, opting to skip watching my favorite show, *Family Matters.* The antics of Steve Urkel were not going to be amusing that evening. I checked the position of the knife, closed my eyes, and anticipated my return to school. I contemplated how I would get Ashley back. I felt like the Grinch from *How the Grinch Stole Christmas,* hatching his plan to steal everything from the residents of Who-ville.

I was abruptly awakened from my peaceful sleep by my uncle standing over my bed with his pants unfastened. I tried to act like I was sleeping, but my heart was beating a mile a minute in my chest as I gripped the knife under my pillow.

"Little bitch, I know you not sleep. Open up for Uncle Darryl ," he said as he dropped his pants to his ankles and stepped out of one pants leg before moving to climb on top of me.

Just as he settled on the side of the bed, I jumped up and put him in a headlock, pressing the knife blade to his throat.

"We're not doing this anymore, you hear me? We're family, and this shit just ain't right," I said to him as the knife began to dig into his flesh on the side of his neck. He was sweating bullets as he tried to breathe with me pressing on his esophagus.

"Baby girl, I just came to give you your allowance and thank you for dinner," he said as he tried to catch his breath. I'm sure he didn't expect me to snap the way I did. He was really trying to hit it before he went to sleep.

"Look, I'm tired of sleeping with one eye open. Why bring these women here and not sleep with them?"

"Baby girl, let me . . ."

"Don't 'baby girl' me. This shit is coming to an end tonight. Make this your last trip to my room."

I held the knife to his back as he eased off the bed. When he got to the door he took a few bills out of his wallet and placed them on my dresser before closing the bedroom door behind him. I breathed a sigh of relief as I lay back in my bed and put my knife back under my pillow. When I woke up in the morning, Uncle Darryl was gone, but the money he left was still on the dresser. I counted two hundred dollars total.

Taking my time in the shower, I put on one of the new outfits I bought the day before and combed my hair down as I had seen my mother do. Adding the money my uncle gave me to the change I had from the day before, I stopped at the corner store to buy a lock for my door and purchased a bottle of Nair hair removal lotion.

By the time I got to school my confidence level was through the roof as I strutted through the halls like I owned them. Removing the remaining condoms from my locker and gathering the books I needed for second period, I made my way to the girls' locker room so I could get ready for first period gym.

Ashley and her crew looked at me oddly and laughed at their own jokes, hoping to make me feel self-conscious. I paid them no attention as I took off my new jeans and shirt, folded them neatly so they wouldn't wrinkle, and then changed into my blue gym suit. I applied a small amount of lip gloss to my already shiny lips. Brushing my soft hair into a ponytail so I wouldn't sweat out my wrap, I looked in the mirror one last time before sitting on the bench to change my shoes. I waited until I was the last one in the locker room before putting my plan into action.

Every Tuesday like clockwork, Ashley washed her hair, leaving it curly for the rest of the day. I laughed to myself as I poured half the contents of her shampoo bottle down the drain before replacing it with the Nair. After shaking it up vigorously, I placed it back into Ashley's locker and put the bottle of Nair in the bottom of my book bag. Tossing everything back into my locker, I made sure to put the combination lock on before heading to join the class with a bright smile on my face,

During gym, I heard all of the little giggles and sly remarks from Ashley and the gang, but I just chilled and smiled, knowing I would have the last laugh. I breezed through the exercises and was the only girl able to climb all the way up the rope and ring the bell. I noticed the stares I got from the boys in my class as they watched my ass bounce in my gym suit, but I paid them no mind. I had a mission to accomplish. Before long, gym was over and it was time to hit the showers.

Casting my shyness to the side and removing all my clothes, I put the plastic cap on my head the way the girl at the store showed me so my hair wouldn't get wet. Moving toward the showers, I made sure to get one near Ashley so I could watch everything take place.

I hung my towel on the hook under the showerhead so it wouldn't get wet and began to soap my body as I discreetly watched Ashley get into the shower. Getting a quick peek at her body before she closed the shower stall door that came up to just above her breasts, I saw that she had a nice pair of breasts—at least a 36C. I looked down at my A cups, then briefly glanced back at her.

I watched as she closed her eyes and put her head under the showerhead, soaking her hair so she could apply what she thought was shampoo. Before I could turn my head she caught me looking at her. My heart was beating fast as hell as she poured a huge amount of the concoction I made into her hair.

"Damn, what the fuck, are you lesbian now? First you fuck my man, now you wanna fuck me?"

Instead of responding, I rinsed my body under the water and lathered up again as she worked her hands through her hair with her eyes closed. When she stepped back under the water big sections of her hair slid off her scalp and ran down her body. She was oblivious because her eyes were closed. I turned my back to her, not quite believing that my plan had actually worked. She applied more of my concoction to her hair with her eyes still closed, and began to lather her hair again.

I was cracking up on the inside as clumps of her hair slid down her body. When she opened her eyes, clumps of hair were in her hands, and even more was at her feet. Ashley began screaming at the top of her lungs, causing a crowd of naked teenage girls to gather around her. The more she rinsed, the more her hair came out, causing Ashley to collapse in a crying heap on the floor.

Ms. Rhodes, our gym teacher, came to see what all the commotion was about. When she walked in she began screaming, asking us what happened and wrapping a towel around Ashley's head and body, calling the principal on her walkie-talkie for help. We were instructed to get dressed and immediately report to second period class. I kept my mouth shut, although I wanted to jump for joy at my silent victory. *One down, many more to go,* I thought.

Before the school day was over we received letters to take

home to our parents explaining what had happened to Ashley, and to inform them that we would be taking gym last period because they were banning shower use at the school. I practically skipped out the school and all the way up the strip to get some more outfits and accessories for school.

When I walked into the house, Uncle Darryl wasn't home yet, giving me time to stash my newest purchases in the closet and put the new lock on my door. When I walked into the room, I was shocked to discover that Uncle Darryl had purchased me a new and bigger bed to sleep in. The comforter and sheets on the bed matched the curtains.

My little black and white television was replaced with a nineteen-inch color television with a remote. When I opened my closet a few of my old clothes were thrown out and my new clothes were hanging in their place, and my new shoes were lined up on the top of the closet. When I reached in the back my jar was still there, but when I counted my stash I had seven hundred dollars in it and I had taken three hundred out just the day before.

When I sat down on my bed I was surprised to find the knife still there. Under the other pillow was a note from someone named Stephanie telling me to find another hiding place for my jar, and to keep the knife in my room just in case. My uncle told her what I did to him and she helped him redecorate my room as a means of apology. I felt tears well up in my eyes at the gesture, and I did what she said.

Looking around my room, I noticed tons of new things, like the vanity that sat by my closet full of perfumes and feminine products, and an electric crimping iron accompanied by my new flat iron. I even had new clothes baskets, one for coloreds and one for whites. For the first time in my life I felt like a teenager should.

I raced downstairs and began to cook dinner so I could be done in time to watch a little television before I went to bed. I placed the bottle of Nair on my vanity and tossed the note from school in the trash. When I heard my uncle come in, I noticed he was with the lady from the other night. After fixing their plates, she winked at me before I went to clean the kitchen, letting me know she had my back. On my way upstairs my uncle stopped me before I reached the steps.

"Baby girl, I hope you liked your—"

"Darryl, leave the girl alone. She's cool. Right, Monica?"

"Uhhh . . . right. Thanks," I replied, shocked that she knew my name. She winked at me again before I went upstairs, and for the first night in a long time I felt at peace, even though I was almost certain it would be short lived.

That night I lay in my bed thinking of how I could get Kevin back. My plan was almost perfect. It would take me the rest of the week, but he had it coming. When I finally went to sleep I had a dream that I was in the shower at school, only my head was attached to Ashley's body. I was leaned up against the stall wall as she knelt down under the shower with her face between my legs. She was orally pleasing me beyond my wildest dreams, but as the water ran over her head, her hair was sliding off. I wanted to stop her, but she had my clit in her mouth and her fingers in my pussy, causing me to explode in one orgasm after another. I didn't know what the dream meant, but I smiled despite the situation.

On Friday I was ready to set my plan with Kevin into action. After this he would surely think twice before violating another woman again. I left a note for him to meet me at the same spot behind the bleachers on Sunday evening. I had to play my part, so I wore one of the new miniskirts I'd purchased, and a fitted shirt that showed my belly button. I made sure my hair was freshly flat ironed, and my lips were shining.

I was a little nervous about him not being there, but smiled instantly when I saw his car parked on the side of the gate by the field. I kept my bag close to me because I needed

the contents if this plan was going to work. His face held a
bright smile as I walked closer to him.

"Follow me. I got something to show you." I didn't bother
to wait for him. I started walking toward the school as he
scrambled to catch up with me.

On Sunday afternoons the side door was always open because they had adult GED training for a couple of hours. I
led him into the building quietly and upstairs to our home-
room class. Giving him full view of my bare bottom with my
ass perched on the teacher's desk, I could see his arousal
from the chair he sat in. Walking seductively toward him, I
straddled his lap and gyrated my hips on his stiffness, the
warmth from my opening heating his length.

I kissed his lips, slipping the two GHB pills I paid a smoker
to get from the drug house around the corner from my
house from under my tongue and into his mouth. He swallowed them without a second thought. Continuing to move
my hips, I eased his manhood out of his pants, rubbing it
against my clit, but not allowing him to penetrate me.

Pretty soon the effects of the pills caused his eyelids to get
heavy and his body to slump in the chair. Once he was completely out I went to work, stripping him naked and chaining
his hands and feet to the teacher's chair. Class would start at
7:15 a.m., just in time for the pill to stop working and Prince
Charming to wake up. I nailed the wooden legs of the chair
to the old hardwood floor so it wouldn't topple over. Once
Kevin's limp body was secure in the seat, I took a permanent
black magic marker and wrote, "I AM A RAPIST" in big,
bold letters all over his body, starting at his forehead and
working my way down until his entire body was covered. I
then Krazy-glued the outline of his feet to the floor. Once
outside, I drove his car to the middle of the football field
and spray painted the word RAPIST all over the inside and
outside of his car, and left it running.

When I got to class in the morning a huge crowd was

standing outside the door as the school principal, the school nurse, and the security guard worked to get Kevin unstuck and unlocked. They kept asking him who did this to him, but he kept his mouth shut as we made eye contact from my position in the hallway.

This fiasco made the local papers that evening with photos of his car and of him being led out of the school in a bathrobe on the first page. One more student out of school for the week. I was almost satisfied, but I had one more to go.

Carlos

Family Ties: Present Day

I had it all figured out by the time Thursday rolled around. I would spend the weekend with Yoyo and force her to tell me everything I needed to know about Monica. Besides, Yoyo was the type who would sell out God himself if Satan offered her enough dope to snort. She didn't give a damn about her family, and she made it known. She once told me that the only thing family was good for was giving her money and getting her out of jams.

So, late Friday afternoon, after I made sure my right hand man knew how to get at me if need be, I was off the scene and smiling up in Yolanda's face. She opened the door, and to my surprise, she was fully dressed. When I stepped into her place, she gave me a hug, then went back to watching television without saying a word.

Not knowing what to think, I hung my coat up in the closet and took a seat next to her on her sofa. My instincts told me to just get my shit and bounce, but I needed some info from her. We sat in silence for about ten minutes before I spoke.

"Yolanda, are you . . ."

"Hush nigga, damn. I'm trying to figure out the puzzle," she replied, sounding irritated and never taking her attention away from the screen. I wanted to jump in her ass for screaming at me, but I had to be nice to her if I wanted her to tell me what I needed to know.

When the show was over, she finally gave me her attention. I didn't know if she was getting high before I got there, but I was not in the mood for her bullshit. Yoyo could be a bitch sometimes, and I was hoping that day wasn't one of those days.

"So wassup, Carlos? What brings you to my neck of the woods?" she asked as if she didn't just snap on me a moment ago. I was close to smacking her ass up, but I wasn't in the mood for fighting with her.

"Damn, ma, can I miss you? It's been a while since I've been through this way. How you been?"

"I'm good. You know how I do."

She stood up to stretch, my eyes catching every curve. Her ass bounced in her jeans as she pranced around the living room. She could have easily been an Apple Bottoms model. Yoyo was a damn dime from head to toe. She had the same smooth chocolate skin like her sister, but she had a little more thickness to her which filled out her jeans perfectly. Just the thought of her ass bouncing on my dick had me ready to bend her over the back of the couch, but I held it down. We'd get to that later.

"How's ya family?"

"My family?" she turned around stunned, like I had just asked her to kill for me.

I knew asking her that would stop her dead in her tracks. Everyone knew she didn't get down with her peoples like that. It was almost a sin to even bring it up in a conversation, but I knew she at least kept in touch with Monica. She was in and out of the pen too much not to have a source of help.

"Yes, your family. You know . . . your brother, Brian, and

your sister, Monica. When was the last time you talked to her, by the way?" I was hoping it was recently.

"You know Brian don't fuck with us. And Monica be on some ol' other shit. I only call that bitch when I need to get out of a jam. Why, you tryna fuck her too?"

"Did I say all that?"

"You didn't have to. Now that your boy is out of the picture you can slide on in. She likes 'get money' niggas like you."

"Oh, so you brushin' me off? Ya family can get at me like that? I thought me and you were tight?" I asked, feigning like I was hurt. Yolanda obviously knew something I didn't, but I knew she would never just come out and say it.

"Yeah, we thick as thieves," she replied sarcastically with a smirk on her face. I knew what it was hittin' for, and her facial expression let me know she wasn't falling for the okey-doke. "So what do you need me to do, or do you need me to find out some shit?"

"Damn, ma, you killin' me."

"I ain't killing you, I'm keeping it real. The only time you blow through here is when you want something, be it ass or info."

"Yoyo, you know it's not even like that." I got up and went over to where she was standing so I could look her in the eyes. Even though we both knew it was bullshit, I wanted to at least sound sincere. "You just always seem to have some info I can use, and you ride out for me. I know I always got you in my corner, ma."

"Is that so? So why are you here today?"

"Because I missed you . . ."

"And?"

"I need some info on ya sister."

"See, I knew it was some bullshit!" Yolanda said, breaking from my embrace. I tried to pull her back, but she was already turned around and facing me.

"What bullshit, Yoyo?"

"You only here to get the scoop on my people. You only using me!"

"And you're not using me? Did you forget so soon the price I have to pay to get what I want? Eight balls ain't cheap, or are you getting ya nose candy from someone else nowadays?"

That hushed her ass right on up. She stood there looking at me for a minute like she was contemplating a way to kill me, but then she plastered a fake ass smile on her face like everything was cool. I watched as she went around the room turning out the lights and the television before I followed her back to her room.

She immediately began to undress when we reached her bedroom, her back facing me the entire time. I stretched out across her bed and watched, wondering when she had become so shy. Shit, this was the same chick who answered the door asshole naked on any given occasion, so why the sudden case of shyness now? I didn't even bother to ask as I watched her do her thing while I chilled fully clothed in her bed. She'd be working for the dick that night, for sure.

Yoyo wrapped a towel around her body before she went into the bathroom to turn the shower on. Normally I would be naked and in there with her, but I just fell back and clicked on the television. She was stubborn, and I damn sure wasn't going to make it easy.

Forty-five minutes went by before she came back into the bedroom, and by then I was already sleepy. I watched her dry off through half-closed eyelids, feigning sleep while she started undressing me. I cooperated as she removed every stitch of clothing from my body with lightning speed.

Yoyo wasted no time getting into position and squatting down on the head of my dick. She was killing the game as she rotated between riding just the head and taking all ten inches. I swear this girl needed to bottle some of that shit because the pussy was tight.

"So, why are you here, Carlos? What do you want from me, huh?" Yolanda asked as she grinded her pelvis into mine, causing my toes to curl up from the grip her walls had on me.

"I . . . I need some . . . damn, girl," I could hardly get it out. She was doing the damn thing to me with her legs wrapped around my back pulling me closer to her with each stroke.

"What you need, boo? Talk to me."

"I need . . . I need some info on Monica."

"What kind of info?" she asked as she rotated her body so her back was facing me. I loved the view of my dick going in and out of her. I had to look away before I messed around and ended it all.

"What happened with Rico, and what really went down with the police. He was untouchable until she came along."

"I see, so what you gonna do for me?"

Instead of responding, I met her stroke with a hard thrust, causing her to moan louder. Quickly gaining control of the situation, I picked her up off me so she could lie back on the bed and I tore the pussy up. We pushed and pulled on each other until it was over for both of us.

When we were done, Yolanda retrieved the eight ball from my pants pocket, tucking it in her nightstand. I made myself comfy on the bed as Yolanda got a warm rag from the bathroom. I was excited but I kept my cool because I didn't want to let on how important this info was to me.

"Well, since you've been so nice to me I'll see what I can come up with. Just give me a couple days, but for now let me see what my loving sister is up to."

Monica

Pandora's Box

"OK, Ms. Tyler, you are about twenty-three weeks pregnant and everything is looking good so far. Because of your past medical history, I'll be placing you as a high risk pregnancy until further notice, just to make sure everything is running smoothly. I need you to fill out these forms, and . . ."

The nurse must have gone on forever until I tuned her out. Honestly, I couldn't really focus on anything else after she told me how far along I was. Twenty-three weeks . . . that was almost six months pregnant. The crazy thing was I really had to put my plan into action before I started showing. Right then I had a little pooch, but you know how that could go. One day I'd be fitting my clothes, and the next I'd be big as hell.

I shook my head and gave her one word answers as I signed my life away on the papers she placed in front of me. I knew for sure that once this baby dropped, my ass would be right back in the gym, and I hoped to God I didn't get stretch marks. If only I could let this baby grow in a jar or something, I'd promise I'd come back to get it when it was ready. Hell, who was I kidding? This wouldn't be easy, but the sooner it was over, the better. And I couldn't wait to get back to the gym to confirm if the rumor that I had been hearing was true or not. Rumor had it that the twins from the gym had ran up in Jasmine at her crib while James wasn't home. I couldn't wait to drop this baby just to get the scoop straight from the horses' mouths about this one. It sounded like it might be just the thing I could use to finally tear Jazz and James apart. If my pregnancy alone wouldn't do it, I knew that there isn't a married man alive who would stay with his wife after two guys ran a train on her ass!

"Ms. Tyler, I asked you a question," the nurse snapped, annoyed that I was ignoring her.

"Oh, I'm sorry. I just have a lot on my mind. Can you ask your question again?"

"Will the child's father be joining you in Lamaze class, or will you be partnering with someone else?" she asked as she glanced at me over the top of her glasses, noting my chart at the same time.

"Ummm . . . no, I'll be attending by myself. My fiancé is extremely busy."

"Do you have a girlfriend or a family member who can come with you? You need to be partnered up."

"I said no," I responded, getting frustrated that she felt the need to constantly remind me of my predicament.

"Well, I'll see if we can partner you with one of the assistants at the facility," she replied hurriedly as she gathered the papers in a sloppy pile. She had just a little too much attitude for me, and I really wasn't in the mood for being pleasant.

"You can get dressed now. Make an appointment for four weeks from now at the front desk. Do you have any questions?"

"No, not right now."

"OK, Ms. Tyler. I'll see you in a few weeks."

After she closed the door, I stepped down off the exam table to take a look in the mirror before I put my clothes back on. The skin on my belly was still smooth, but I was developing a little pooch from the baby growing inside me. As I turned for a side view I began to feel overwhelmed because my mom wasn't there to share the moment.

I wanted to hate my mom for not being strong enough to stand up for herself. I never met my grandmother, so I didn't know what kind of woman she was, but if my mother was any example of her upbringing, then I'm glad I never met her. I wanted to hate my mother for not protecting me from the hands of my brother and stepfather. Although neither of them ever penetrated me, what they made me do was unspeakable. I knew she heard my cries for help, but she never came.

I wanted to hate her for leaving me and not teaching me what I needed to know to survive, but how could she if she didn't know how to survive herself? I wiped my tears and put my clothes back on. Now wasn't the time for tears. I had things to do, and I couldn't be getting all soft all of a sudden.

After standing in line for all of fifteen minutes to pay my co-payment and schedule my next appointment I was finally on my way out the door. I bumped into some chick on the way out, but I honestly didn't care enough to look back. If I had, maybe I'd have caught the dirty look I'm sure she threw my way, but I was on a mission and probably wouldn't have cared either way.

Getting home in record time I pulled up just in time to see the FedEx delivery guy pull away from my house. I didn't remember ordering anything, but I had to pee so bad it didn't matter. I just threw the damn box on the couch with the rest of my stuff and went to handle my business.

After relieving myself, I made a sandwich before I went back to the couch, pushing the box to the side until I was finished with my meal. It wasn't until I watched a couple of my favorite shows did I decide to finally see what was in the box. I sat it on the table and took careful measures not to shake it up or cut the packing too deep since I didn't know what was inside.

Inside the FedEx box was a beautifully beaded pink box. It had jewels on it, and pink was my favorite color. I was puzzled and excited because I knew I hadn't ordered anything. I briefly wondered who sent it before taking the lid off.

The box smelled sweet as I pulled out the tissue paper that covered whatever was inside. My face went from a look of wonderment to shock as I viewed the contents of the box. Inside I found a little doll dressed in what appeared to be a black dress as if she were mourning. A knife was sticking out of what seemed to be her pregnant stomach. Further inspection produced a headless baby and a little car that looked like a hearse. Black rose petals filled the bottom of the box, and a card sat in the corner.

I was scared to open the card at first, but curiosity was killing me. Inside I found a card that had black roses on the front with a picture of an eye in the middle. The words "I've Got My Eye On You" were typed right across the middle. I put the card down with shaking hands and leaned back on the couch to gather my thoughts. Who would be watching me? Why? I'd done so much dirt in my life that it was hard to tell who'd want to get back at me.

I sat on the couch stunned for what felt like hours. With the exception of Jazz and James, everyone else I did anything to got what they deserved. I didn't force myself on anyone. They came to me willingly. I don't know how long I sat there until the ringing phone startled me out of my thoughts. I hesitated to answer, not sure if I really wanted to talk. The person who sent the package obviously knew where I lived, so who was to say that he or she didn't have my phone number? I crept to the phone, not realizing how crazy

I must have looked. I stood near the phone and allowed it to ring again before I answered.

"Hello?" I answered the phone, my voice barely audible. I don't know what the hell I was so scared of. Killers don't normally call first.

"Hey, big sis! How's it going?"

"Yolanda?"

"Please, call me Yoyo. Besides, how many little sisters do you have?"

"No, it's just that I wasn't expecting your call. Are you locked up again?" Not for nothing, I didn't mind hearing from my sister. I mean, we were family and all, but the only time she called was if she was in a jam or short on cash like I was a damn ATM. I can't even begin to count the number of times I had to help her out. We weren't that close as kids either, with her being a prissy brat, and me having to hold the house down because Lord knows our brother wasn't doing shit to help. I loved her because we were family, but I despised her so much because she had it made.

"Damn, is that the only reason I can have to call you? Hell, I thought we were family."

"And when did family mean anything to you?"

"Look, Moni, I ain't call to argue with you."

"OK, so you're not in jail. What do you need? Money?"

"Damn, Monica, can a bitch call and see how you doing without wanting something? Rico is gone, and you're there by yourself. I'm just calling to check up on you."

"Well, a bitch can surely call to check me out, but I have yet to see a female dog dial a telephone. And since when did you care about anyone's well-being but your own?"

"You know what, Monica, I tried to be civil with your evil ass. You're going to die a lonely, old, bitter bitch. That's why I don't fuck with you now. You've always been a—"

"Yoyo, I'm pregnant." I had to blurt it out before I lost the nerve. For the first time I was actually scared of what was coming. I knew I wasn't anywhere near being the motherly type. What was I going to do?

"What? By who?"

"You don't know him," I said as I walked back to the couch and flopped down. What the hell have I gotten myself into? James didn't want this baby, and since I was keeping it real, neither did I. My dumb ass done got caught up on Jazz's table so I knew that was a done deal, unless . . .

"Do I need to call Maury? He'll test you and all of your baby father possibilities."

"Yolanda, I didn't say I didn't know the father of my child. I said you don't."

"So, what's the problem?"

"I'm not sure if I want to keep it."

"Girl, you better hold it down. Your ass ain't getting any younger, and the least you could do is keep Rico's baby since he ain't here no more."

"Rico? I am not pregnant by Rico. Where you hear that?"

"I just assumed it was his since y'all were kicking it like that. Didn't you feel bad for getting him locked up?"

"First off, I was pregnant before that shit went down with Rico, and what I had with him was strictly business. I didn't know he was going to kill himself."

"So, if it ain't Rico's kid, whose is it?"

"You don't know him."

"Well is he at least claiming the bastard?"

"Yolanda, what did you call here for?"

"Just to see what's up."

"Well if you're done with your twenty questions, I have some phone calls to make."

"One more before you go."

"What?"

"Can we go shopping or something? I need like three hundred dollars, and a new outfit to wear to Fat Daddy's party on

next Saturday night. I saw these Jimmy Choo boots that I just
have to have."

"You said that like you've ever done something for me.
How much is your tab now?"

"Girl, as long as I owe you . . ."

"I won't be broke regardless. Call me next week. I'll meet
you downtown."

"Thanks, Moni. You know I love you, right?"

"Yeah, right. You love me like I love a pair of Payless shoes.
Goodbye."

I didn't wait for a response. I hung up. I had to start setting my plan into action, and I needed the help of a few old
friends. I called Sheila and smiled to myself despite the situation. It'd been a while, and I hadn't heard from her since I
got her that job as the judge's secretary. She owed me a favor
or two.

Sheila S. Stone

I swear, life was such a BITCH sometimes! One day you'd be sitting on top of the world, and the next day your ass would be getting crushed by it. My past had been haunting me like crazy, making it hard for me to move on. I was so mad at myself I didn't know what to do, but at the same time I was stuck between a rock and a hard place. That's why when Monica set me up to work with the judge I hopped right on it. I knew my job with Jazz was over. That's why I didn't even bother to go back and get the stuff I left there. I could do without the memories.

I thought for sure Monica would be calling for me to return the favor, and surprisingly she hadn't yet. I had my guard up, though, because I knew it was coming. I wished I could call Jazz and apologize, but what was I supposed to say? I'm sorry for setting you up and getting caught fucking your husband on your kitchen table? I really did want to talk to her, but I wasn't ready yet.

My phone had been ringing nonstop all morning, and it was working my nerves. The judge was sleeping with half the women in Philly, but I just stayed my ass out of it, took mes-

sages, and smiled brightly when I saw his wife. The last time
I tried to help someone my ass got caught up. I knew whoever this was calling now was persistent. The damn phone
had rung ten times. I had to find a way to change the ring
count so the answering service would pick up after three
rings.

"Good afternoon and thank you for calling District
Council Three. Sheila speaking. How may I help you?"

"Sheila, it's me, Monica. I need to talk to you about something."

Speak of the damn devil . . .

Carlos

The Scoop

"**D**amn, Carlos. For all that you should have called her yourself. You was all up on the phone like you dialed the number."

As soon as Yoyo hung up the phone I was in her ear about Monica. Hopefully she got some info I could use, and they weren't just talking about some girlie bullshit. I tried to go pick up the other line in the kitchen so I could listen, but she wouldn't let me get out of the bed. I even tried to put my face next to hers on the receiver, but she kept pushing me away. As soon as she hung up, I was all in the business asking a million questions.

"So, what she say?"

"Nothing really. She's pregnant, and it's not Rico's."

"Oh word?" Now, I already knew she was pregnant because Shaneka was crying about it earlier this week, but I didn't know it wasn't Rico's baby, which meant Shaneka was spazzing for nothing. She did feel like Rico betrayed her, though, so I'd just keep that bit of info to myself and let her get her shit off.

"So what happened with all that money Rico had?"

"Did it sound like we were able to discuss all that? Hell, you were practically on the phone with her your damn self."

"Well, it's shit like that that I need to know. That man had major chips, and I know she walked away with a nice piece of it."

"Maybe you should write a list of questions so I know what to ask her specifically. That eight you gave me ain't covering any detective work."

"Well, what it cover?"

"Good pussy, nigga. Who fucking you like I do? The information you want I can definitely get, but what do I get out of it?"

"What you talking? Chips?" I was trying to decide if it was worth the money and aggravation. It only took me three seconds to decide it was.

"Major chips, but for right now we have some unfinished business."

I knocked Yoyo off real quick and left. She was upset because we were supposed to be spending the weekend together, but she cheered her ass right up after I promised her a shopping spree. On the real, I had to get back on the block. I totally trusted my right hand man, but just like with me and Rico, a dude got to watch his back because your main man will be the first to do you in. Now that I knew what's good with this Monica chick, I needed something to get Judge Stenton off my damn back.

I pulled up to one of my many safe houses about a half hour later, and apparently right on time. Walking into a heated debate between my main man, Jesus, also known as The God, and his man, Hector, I just took a seat at the table and let them continue as I tried to piece together what was happening.

"That nigga's a fuckin' rat."

"All I'm saying is how the hell that same nigga keep coming up short? Think about it, man."

"You know the block he on is slow. Especially since Rico got knocked."

"Slow ain't got shit to do with counting chips. He's either taking off the top, or he smoking the supply."

I listened to them go back and forth while I grabbed a glass of juice. I made it a rule to always let them handle their own problems, but I knew if I allowed them to continue someone would be lying in blood and I wasn't in the mood.

"So, what exactly happened? Who's the problem?" I asked both men as I took a seat at the table. They looked hesitant to talk and I remained silent until they were ready.

"There's a snake in our camp."

"Who?" They both looked at me, then at each other before responding. I didn't think I would be shocked by who it was, but more hurt by the situation.

"Well," The God began. Looking as if he wasn't sure he wanted to be the one to say it. I surely wasn't going to make the situation any easier.

"It's that fuckin' lowlife-ass, Arturo," Hector blurted out. He was so upset that you could practically see steam coming from his ears. The God just dropped his head in defeat, bracing himself for what was to come.

"God, I thought you had that situation straightened out. Didn't we have a problem with him before?"

"Yeah, but I . . ."

"Fuck all that! He's been fucking up his money for the past six weeks. I told you not to fuck with those young boys. Now look at us," Hector exploded, looking like he was ready to take The God out. Out of all the men I had on my squad, Hector was the main one who was willing to ride or die for me regardless of the situation.

"I told you I'd handle it."

"When? After you finish getting your cut?"

"You calling me a thief?"

"If the vest fits—" Hector's thought was cut short before

he could even finish his sentence. Just that fast The God had snatched him up by his throat. The one thing I could say was this: The God was calm but quick. With him, one second you'd be breathing and the next you'd be meeting your maker. That's why we called him The God. He could give you life or take it away in a heartbeat.

After two grueling minutes, The God finally let Hector's throat go, leaving him gasping for air as he tried to catch his breath. I formed a plan in my head to find out exactly who was doing what. If there was a snake present, his ass would be dead before sunrise.

"We'll meet up here tonight at about nine. Right now I'm going to set the block up to see exactly what's going on." Just for my own curiosity I had to put some eyes on the street to see what the real deal was. There is usually more than one rotten apple in a bunch, and it was time to start weeding them out. I also had to find men I could trust to watch Monica and not try to snake me for their own come up.

"Do you want squad or just us two to come?" The God asked as he took his seat again. I could tell he really wanted to whip Hector's ass. But that could be handled another night.

"For now just us until I see what's what. We'll talk later. Hasta la muerte, que exista honor."

Both men replied in Spanish first, then English, "Till death, let there be honor." We all knew that if Arturo wasn't on point, death would surely come. There was no honor amongst thieves, and no room for shiesty niggas in this game.

Monica

Speak of the Devil

"Sheila, I need a favor."

I knew I was definitely the last person Sheila wanted to hear from, especially since I'd been the sole reason for her demise, but she owed me. If it weren't for me, she wouldn't be in the position she was in. There was no way she would've been able to continue to work with Jazz, so what was she going to do for income? Like I said, she owed me—her life.

"Monica, I was wondering when you were going to call. It's been, what, four months now?"

"Just about, but enough of that. I need a favor."

"I'm done with favors, Monica. That's the reason I'm where I am now."

"You are in a way better position now. Did you really think you were going to advance at that law firm?" Now I was starting to get heated. I had saved her from an awkward situation, and she was making way more money now. Didn't she know who I was?

"It's not about me advancing, it's the principle. Besides, I'm sure you didn't call me to discuss my financial status, so what is it that I need to do now to pay my lifelong debt to you?"

"Oh, so we have a backbone this year. Cool, I'm just calling to see if you could be my partner in Lamaze class. I start next week."

"Lamaze class? You're pregnant?"

"What other reason would I have to go to Lamaze classes?"

"I'm just shocked. I had no idea that you actually got pregnant. Is it James's?"

"Who else's would it be? You know the history." I was getting sick of this conversation with Sheila. We were all on that kitchen table that night, and even before that when we had the first threesome she knew how we got down. So why was she acting all clueless all of a sudden?

"Why would you keep it? You know James is not going to want that baby, and Jazz is going to have a fit."

"Since when did you become president of the Jazz and James fan club? They don't give a damn about you, so why do you care?"

"That's not what I'm saying, Monica. All I'm saying is why bring a child in this world you know you don't want? That child didn't ask to be here."

"So what do you suppose I should do, since you like playing Dr. Fucking Phil? Tell me what I need to be doing." By now I was *extra* pissed. Like I needed her throwing in my face what I was doing. In the back of my mind I knew it wasn't right, but my heart still belonged to Jazz. I just needed to get her to see things my way, that was all.

"All I'm saying is it's cheaper to spend three hundred dollars now, than three million during a lifetime."

"What?"

"Get an abortion, Monica. It's better that way."

"Abortion? Are you serious? Look, I need you to help me at the Lamaze class, and it starts Monday. Will you do it?"

"I'll be there Monday. Where am I meeting you?" She sounded defeated, but ask me if I gave a damn.

"Meet me at the University of Pennsylvania Hospital on the fifth floor. It starts at 4 o'clock."

"I'll be there."

"Of course you will. See you then."

After hanging up I made my way to my room. I was always able to think better in there, and now would be the perfect opportunity to have some alone time. Rico had been on my mind lately, and I needed to find out what went down with him. From what I understood, he hung himself in prison, but my gut was telling me otherwise. Maybe I needed to take a trip up to the prison to see what exactly went down. I didn't want to call the judge again, but who else could get me up there without a problem?

I went past his house, and when I didn't see his wife's car outside I went to ring the bell. His car wasn't there either, but I was hoping maybe his son had it and he was really home. Pulling my cell phone out of my pocketbook, I dialed the judge's number, hoping his wife wouldn't answer. The phone rang five times before the answering machine came on. I didn't bother to leave a message; I just simply called the courthouse. I didn't want Sheila in my business, but she just may prove to be useful later on.

"District Council—"

"Sheila, put Stenton on the phone." I cut her off dead in the middle of her sentence.

"Who may I tell him is calling?"

"Who's calling? Girl, put the judge on the phone. You don't recognize my voice by now?" Sheila didn't answer; she just clicked over immediately. A minute later the judge's deep baritone voice came through the other end of the receiver.

"Monica, long time, no hear. To what do I owe the pleasure of this call today? Do you have the lead on any more drug dealing boyfriends I should know about?" the judge said with a hint of hope under his laughter. Busting Rico put him on the map, and he was rewarded handsomely, despite the money he took up front during the bust.

"Not today, Judge, I just need some info on Rico's stay in prison. I just need to know how he came to hang himself."

"Well, sweetie, I wasn't exactly there to witness it, but the guard on duty at the time said she found him hanging there when she was doing her rounds. He was in the cell by himself, so it was just assumed that he did it himself. Why? Do you think there was someone in there who wanted him gone?"

"He was a damn drug dealer—kingpin to the fullest. Of course there was someone who wanted him dead. Shit, plenty of people were waiting for that. I just need to know who got to him. You and I both know that Rico would never hang himself. Let's be real."

"OK, so what do you want me to do? Have every man in the entire prison put on a lie detector? Monica, you need to explain yourself better than this."

"No, I'll just talk to a few people if you let me, but first I want to talk to the guard. She was the one on duty, so I'm sure they exchanged some kind of conversation."

"Listen, give me a couple of days to set it up for you. I have to clear it with the warden first. I just can't allow you to waltz up in prison and start questioning people. You act like you work for the D.A. or something."

"Do what you have to do, but get back to me by the end of the work day. And don't let the guard know I'm coming. I don't want to give her time to get her story together."

"As you wish, master," the Judge responded in a mock genie voice that almost made me laugh. Almost. "I'll give you a call by six."

"Looking forward to hearing from you."

"Yeah, I'm looking forward to sleeping with you, too." He hung up before I had a chance to respond.

I thought of what I could ask the guard, and not sound like I didn't know what I was talking about. The information she would be giving me could get a ton of people swept off the streets, and I needed to go about getting it the right way so I could make my next move. I raced home to wait for the package from Stenton. I knew this was my only shot at finding out what really happened with Rico, and I had to do it right.

The ringing phone woke me up from my sleep. When I looked at the clock it was six on the dot. *When did I fall asleep?* I hurriedly reached for the phone, hoping it was the judge calling.

"Hello?" I answered, trying to sound alert and not like I had just drooled on the side of my face and had a nasty taste in my mouth.

"Monica, it's me, Stenton. I set the meeting up for tomorrow at ten thirty in the morning. The warden OK'd it, and the guard will just be starting her shift. She will be told to report to . . ."

The judge broke everything down for me on where we would meet and how much time I had to question her. He also told me what I should wear, like he really had to. He sent me a badge from the D.A.'s office via FedEx, and it arrived around seven that evening. He tried to get me to commit to seeing him over the weekend, but I rushed his ass off the phone, telling him I would get back to him soon.

The next morning I was up bright and early and on my way to the prison, stopping like a hundred times to go to the restroom. If being pregnant was like this I swore I would never do it again. I arrived at ten after ten, leaving enough time to go to the restroom once more and be seated in the office before the guard got there. I had a list of questions I would ask her and a small tape recorder.

At ten thirty the guard walked in looking like a deer

caught in headlights. I had to give it to Rico, she was a pretty woman. A little on the shy side, but she was pretty.

The second thing I noticed when she walked in was her protruding belly. I didn't know if it was a beer gut or if she was pregnant, but I would find out in time. She said nothing, just sat down in front of me with a scared-ass look on her face and her hands folded across her stomach. She wouldn't look me in the eye, though. Her eyes shot around the room like she couldn't focus—nervous energy. The eyes told everything.

"My name is Samantha, and I just have a few questions for you. I will be recording our conversation, and if necessary this tape will be used in a court of law. Any answers you give need to be accurate to the best of your knowledge. Do you have any questions?" I spoke to her clearly and precisely, opting to use an alias just in case she had heard something about me.

"No . . . no I don't." Her voice was shaky.

"OK, there's no need to be nervous. Just answer the questions to the best of your ability. I will be starting the recording now."

She looked like her heart would burst out of her chest and sprint halfway across town. I kept a straight face and questioned her like I was a damned detective.

"State your name for the record."

"Alexis Cook."

"How long have you been working in this facility?"

"Four years."

"What did you know about Enrique Casarez?"

She didn't answer right away. She sighed and held her breath like she was trying to hold back tears. I didn't know what all that emotion was about. Rico was only in jail for two months before he was found dead, so what kind of relationship could they have had?

"We only spoke a couple of times when he needed to use the phone. I would let him use the one in the supervisor's office. I knew about Rico way before he got here from what people said on the street and from what I saw the few times I saw him on the block. He seemed like a cool guy, so I didn't see the harm in letting him make a call."

"Who did he call? What was he talking about?"

"Well, it sounded like he was calling friends of his. He said something about being set up, but I really wasn't paying attention. While Rico would talk on the phone I would ride him backward until I came. That was my payment for me letting him use the phone."

"What about the setup? Do you know who was setting him up?"

"I'm not really sure. He mentioned some woman's name, and was telling a friend that he thought she was the reason why he got locked up."

"When did y'all last talk? Share what you feel comfortable in telling me, I just need to know the circumstances surrounding his death, and anything too personal will stay between me and you. I just need you to be as honest as possible."

"The last time we talked was right before Juan, or the Cage as we call him, gave me a letter to give to Rico. He found out some information and wanted me to pass the letter to Rico. I was going to see Rico anyway because I found out I was pregnant, and I wanted him to know he would be a daddy. When I got there he was hanging from the ceiling."

"Do you still have the letter?"

"Yeah, it's in my purse in my locker. If you'd like I can go get it for you."

"Sure, you can get it after the interview. How many months are you?"

"I'm sixteen weeks pregnant. I just found out I'm having a boy yesterday."

"OK, thanks for your time, Alexis. You can go get the letter now."

I watched her walk out of the room. I was taking notes as we talked, but I would definitely be listening to the tape when I got home. By the time she came back I had already put everything in my bag, and was standing. She gave me the note and her phone number. She said if I needed to know anything else to give her a call.

When I got out to the car I unfolded the letter and began reading. Apparently, Rico felt I had something to do with his set up and got in contact with Carlos to investigate. I drove home in silence trying to decide what angle I would use to get at Carlos. I would definitely go see the judge to give him the info I had because my ass might need some witness protection after this. For now I was on my way to the Cinque household. If I waited on them they would never talk to me.

Jasmine

Truth Be Told

Iwas released from the hospital three days later with well wishes from the staff, tons of literature to look at for my pregnancy, and a whole lot of stress and anxiety thinking about what I was gonna do since I was carrying twins from what was literally a late morning quickie with two guys I hardly even knew.

At three months, I had a ways to go before I would begin buying anything, and I hoped that the time would go by as quickly as possible. I still couldn't believe I was pregnant with another set of twins, and I couldn't help but wonder how Jalil and Jaden would feel. But for obvious reasons, that was the least of my worries. Yes, it had just been them for the last four years. They were not accustomed to competing with other kids for our attention, but I was sure that wasn't the only problems I was facing. My mind was all over the place. I had to plan their birthday party in another two months, and Lord knew I didn't feel like being around a bunch of kids with a huge belly.

James had been extra attentive, but I was still not open to him. Yeah, I had now probably fucked up a whole lot worse

than he had, but I was still bitter about everything that had
went down between Sheila, James, and Monica.

Truth be told, I was ready to go home, but not to the
home I already had. I was ready to start our life in a new
place, but we had just bought our house five years ago.
Although the events of late were overwhelming, we had so
many memories in that house. I didn't know when, if ever,
I'd get past it.

I'd never prayed so much in my life. It was funny how pre-
viously I had reserved prayer for bedtime and meals, never
calling on God for anything. Now, praying was all I'd been
doing lately. It's true what they say: when he's not walking by
your side, he's carrying you through.

I still saw the image of Monica, Sheila, and James on my
table when I walked in the door, but it was becoming a mere
shadow, not as vibrant as my first time back home. The
voices were getting quieter, and I truly did think we'd get
through this. We had to. We had children to consider. But
what was weird is that I had begun to replay the sexual payback stunt that I had pulled with Donnie and Rahmel.
Damn! It had felt good getting fucked by two men at the same
time, but I knew in many ways I would forever be cursed by
that act of revenge.

James and I weren't in the house for two minutes before
someone was ringing the doorbell. James made sure I was
comfortable on the couch before he went to answer the
door. I propped my feet up on a few pillows and leaned my
head back on the arm rest so I could rest my eyes for a few
seconds. I was considering going to get the kids from my
brother's house so all of us could stay the night with James.
Inching back in slowly but surely was easier. That way if I decided to bail, it wouldn't be too hard.

For a second it sounded like James was arguing with someone at the door, but I wasn't really sure. I heard a female
voice get loud, and I almost lost it. His lover had the nerve to

come here? I got up off the couch and made my way to the door only to receive the shock of my life.

"Monica, what are you doing here?" I had to force myself to keep my mouth from hanging wide open. I wanted to see her, but not now. The pain was still too new.

"Jazz, I came to apologize to both of you, and to talk to you personally. I just figured the longer we. waited, the harder it would become to get past this problem. I wanted you to hear my side of the story."

Before I could say anything James was pushing me back into the house and closing the door. Monica just stood there like she was about to cry, but I held the door just before it closed shut. I had to hear what she had to say.

"James, we should at least hear her out."

"Baby, I don't want that woman in my house. She's the reason why we're in the shit we're in."

"No, you wanting to be greedy is the reason why we're in this shit. Open the damn door. We need closure."

I knew this could be the biggest mistake I ever made in my life, but I needed to hear what she had to say. Maybe if I looked her in the eye, I could understand how she had so much power over people to make them do things they really didn't want to do. There was no denying her skills in the bedroom. On that note she was a phenomenal woman. When she was around you couldn't think rationally. For my own curiosity, I just needed to know.

"You better make this quick, and make this your last damn visit. You're not welcome here," James said to her as I walked away from the door and resumed my position on the sofa. I didn't offer her a drink or anything because I didn't want her to get comfortable. She needed to state her purpose and keep it moving.

"Monica, what brings you here today?" As she made herself comfortable on the loveseat, I noticed the bulge in her shirt. It could easily be overlooked if you weren't looking for it, but I was dead on it. This bitch was pregnant by my husband, or so we assumed.

"Jazz, first I want to apologize for all the problems I've caused your family. I should have gone about trying to get you in a better manner."

James and I looked at each other and back at her. I didn't think she would come right out and say that she wanted me. I thought for sure she would deny it and take it to her grave, but then again, Monica never failed to amaze me.

"So, you're saying what exactly?"

"I'm saying that I fell in love with you the very first time I saw you, and I thought if I could get close to you maybe I would have a chance. Sheila put it in my head that I could get you if I tried hard enough. She set everything up from the beginning. It was her idea to come here. I would have never thought of it. I could have easily had either of you over at my house."

Still speechless, James and I sat wide-eyed and stared at her like she was a television set. I couldn't believe what she was saying, and if I wasn't there to hear it, no one could have ever convinced me.

"So Sheila put it in your head that it was cool to climb your ass up on my table? Better yet, tell me, Monica, how many times did you and James see each other before I became involved?" I had agreed to move past that, but something was telling me that James wasn't being straight with me. That was our biggest problem, the fact that we were never straight up with each other. But oh well, I still needed to hear it from the horse's mouth.

"We started seeing each other maybe six weeks before he finally decided he would ask you, but we slept together at least thirty times before that night. James couldn't get enough of me."

"And since that night?" I don't think I really wanted to know the answer, but my mouth said it anyway. A part of me did want to know, but another part would rather do without the details.

"We got together at least twice a week. Sheila had him too."

James just put his head down in his hands and shook it from side to side. My breathing felt labored, but I needed to know one more thing.

"Monica, how many months are you?"

"About five-and-a-half."

Before I had a chance to react, James jumped up off the couch beside me and knocked Monica backward out of the chair. By the time I got up he had already punched her in her face once, and I had to practically jump on his back to keep him from swinging again. I don't know where the strength came from, but I was able to pull him up and stand between them so Monica could get up off the floor. She looked stunned, and even though I hated her, I hoped nothing happened to her or her baby. It wasn't the child's fault.

"Get the fuck out of my house! Get the fuck out!" James kept yelling it at the top of his lungs as Monica made her way to the door slowly.

"Jazz, don't be mad at James. He was at my house as much as you were."

Now it was James's turn to hold me as I charged at her like a bull. She was able to open and shut the door before I could get to her, and by the time I got the door open I could see her making her way to her car. She turned and looked at me and stopped me dead in my tracks with her words.

"Oh Jasmine, I forgot to mention that you really look good since I last saw you. I don't know what it is, but maybe it's those *private personal training sessions* that you've been having at your house with the twins Donnie and Rahmel from Bally's. Girl, whatever you do, keep those personal one-on-one sessions going because they really got your body looking tight!"

After she said that there was dead silence as I could not believe that those bitch ass twins from the gym had opened up their mouths and gossiped like straight up bitches!

I wanted to literally kill Monica for having pulled my card like that. But I had to give it up to her, the bitch was vindictive as hell and she was good at it.

James looked at me with a confused look on his face.

I shook my head and asked "What the hell is she talking about?"

Then all I could hear was her car screeching down the street. I just fell to my knees in the doorway and cried, not knowing what to do next. I would be paying her ass a visit. That was for sure. I just hoped I could be civil when I saw her again. Yeah, we were all at fault, but this entire situation just pissed me off. I was hoping that James didn't question me about what Monica had said about the twins training me.

Thankfully, somehow we made our way up to the bedroom where we lay in silence for what felt like hours. I don't know if either of us was ready for what was said, especially me. I was upset that she put James out there, but I was even more upset that she told him my business. And I was even more livid with the twins from Bally's.

Yeah, I had already told James what I wanted him to know, and I'm sure he did the same, but I guess now he knew where all of my panties had been disappearing to.

As I lay next to my husband, I tried to think of what my parents would do in a situation like this. My heart was telling me they would stay together. I needed to move back home. This incident would stay between us, and it was as simple as that. And I would keep my sins a secret for as long as I could.

I rolled over to face James, and he looked just as lost as I did. The only way to get our marriage back on track was for me to move back home and deal with our problems together.

Monica

Revenge Is Best Served Cold, August 1991

When I woke up, the pain in my stomach was unbearable. It definitely didn't feel like the usual menstrual cramps, but what else could it be? I could barely lift my head off the pillow, and when I was able to, and I saw the amount of blood on the bed, it scared me even more. Something wasn't right, and I needed to get help as soon as possible.

I tried to stand up, but my legs felt like wet noodles under me. The pain was getting worse by the second, and all I remember was making it halfway down the hall on my hands and knees before I passed out. Waking up in the emergency room, I was scared for real. I wanted to ask what had happened, but the pain in my stomach and the tubes down my throat prevented me from speaking.

I kept my eyes closed as I listened to my uncle and Stephanie argue about who was going to clean the blood up in the hallway. He wanted me to do it, but she said I wasn't feeling well enough. I hated him, and I couldn't wait to get out of his house. Instead of dwelling on their nonsense I closed my eyes and sifted through my own issues.

* * *

By the end of the school year I had successfully gotten even with two other girls from Ashley's crew: Jessica and Samantha. How I caught Jessica was priceless. Since Ashley and Kevin hadn't returned back to school, the school staff took it upon themselves to plan our junior prom. I was cool with that and happy because I was finally able to talk my uncle into letting me go.

Although I had about twelve hundred dollars stashed in my closet, I still took on a few after-school babysitting jobs to get some extra loot so I wouldn't spend all my money getting what I needed. I decided I would go to the prom by myself. After all my efforts to raise cash, Stephanie offered to take me to New York to get my gown so no one would have one like mine. My gown fell right above my knees and went up around my neck like a halter top. I had a detachable train that fell to the floor and doubled as a shawl just in case I got cold during the night. We bought my shoes and handbag from the same boutique, and I decided on a single pink rose to match my dress for my corsage.

She took me to the guy who did her hair, and taught me how to apply my makeup properly so it would have a natural look. My uncle rented a Benz for the evening, after arguing with Stephanie about it for three days straight, and he decided that since she wanted to be so helpful, Stephanie could take me to the prom and pick me up when it was all over.

To lower the ticket cost, the prom was held in the school gymnasium, which made it convenient for everyone. I had butterflies in my stomach something serious because this was my opportunity to get Jessica's ass. I knew she would come to the prom like she was the shit, and I'd make it my business to show her she was, literally.

I was dropped off at the prom about an hour after it started. I got there just in time to get my picture taken before the camera crew packed up for the evening. Once the prom got popping I went to the ladies' room to make sure the coast was clear. The day before I'd stashed a bag of items in the bathroom vent.

I put "out of order" signs on the stall doors on the ends so that the only restroom available was the middle stall. After hiding my bag in the first stall, I left the bathroom and waited for Jessica to come in. When I saw her go to the bathroom, I waited for a minute before I went in and locked the door behind us.

She was standing at the mirror on the other side when I walked in, so I snuck into the stall and circled the toilet seat with clear super glue. I went into the first stall after using a towel to crawl under the door. Just as I hoped, she walked in and plopped her nasty ass right down on the toilet seat. I took the cup I had in my bag and filled it with water from the toilet. After taking a peek over the top to see what she was doing, I tossed the cup of water over the top.

She screamed as I threw three more cups of water on her. When she realized she couldn't get off the toilet I took the opportunity to crawl back under the door, depositing my bag back in the vent and exiting the bathroom unnoticed.

While I was getting some punch I saw a crowd of students running toward the bathroom. I made my way over, almost the last one there. From my viewpoint I could see Jessica still trying to get off the toilet with her dress and hair drenched, and her panties around her ankles. I should have pissed in the cup.

When we got back to school the following Monday, the school paper was passed out during lunch. On the cover, much to everyone's surprise, was a picture of Jessica stuck on the toilet looking a hot mess. I just laughed to myself as I finished eating my lunch in silence. For the first time in all of my sixteen years I could honestly say life was good.

* * *

Opening my eyes for a brief second I saw the doctor who was working on me. He was telling my uncle that I was pregnant in my tubes and the tube burst, which was the reason for all the pain and blood. I was grateful, but not really. I was upset about the tube part, but if I had the baby who was to say it didn't belong to my uncle? And that shit that Kevin and his boys did still gave me bad dreams, so I was glad it was gone.

I heard the doctor whisper that although the tube was repaired, I wouldn't be able to pass eggs on that side, so it would be a little difficult for me to conceive again. My dumb ass uncle asked the doctor if they could give me a hysterectomy, but of course they wouldn't do it. The effects of the morphine were making me sleepy again, so I let it do its magic as I thought about my revenge on Samantha.

* * *

We were having a festival at our school for our last day. I volunteered to help set the yard up for the fair. In the back of our school there were woods that some of us usually cut through to get to the strip quicker. Jessica wasn't in school to walk home with Samantha, and the rest of her girls went the other way, so I knew if I was going to get her I had to act quickly.

I snuck off while the other volunteers weren't looking and hid my book bag in the woods. Inside my bag I had stuffed my uncle's overall jumpsuit so I wouldn't mess up my clothes, a bandana to cover my face, and a pair of Timberland boots. I had some rope, duct tape, a pack of cigarettes, a jar of honey, and a rechargeable pair of clippers so I didn't need a plug. Her ass was going to catch it, and I couldn't wait.

The day of the festival was hot, but not the type that carried high humidity. I had on my booty-hugging shorts, and a matching red and yellow tank top that looked nice on my tanned skin. My body had filled out a lot in the past couple of months. I had Stephanie take me back to her stylist to get my hair done for the day. I wanted to be cute from head to toe. I finished my outfit off with a pair of red, low top, classic Reeboks and yellow socks with red balls on the back. I must say I was looking rather tasty.

I noticed how the boys in my class had been watching me

lately, but wasn't shit poppin'. After that mess with Kevin, I decided that not another soul in this school would get within sniffing distance of this stuff. I took the compliments they dished out and kept it moving. There was no need for small talk.

I chilled the entire day playing the games and getting my fill of hot dogs, cotton candy, and soda. I flirted with some of the guys, and kept my lips glossy just to make the girls mad. I made sure to keep close tabs on Samantha, and when she left I was right behind her.

I kept ten paces behind her, ducking behind trees to make sure she didn't see me. I had a padlock and four heavy rocks in a sock that I had gathered together before I left the fair. I knew I would have to knock her ass out to tie her to the tree, and I was sure that would do the job. Just as she was about to step over the old tree that lay on the ground, I ran up on her and knocked her in the back of her head. Her body folded like a paper bag.

I left her there while I fished my bag out the hollow part of the tree, shaking the bugs off before I put my overalls on over the outfit I had on and stuck the honey and clippers in my pocket, putting my sneakers inside the bag and placing the bag back in the log. Taking Samantha by her ankles, I dragged her body over to the tree.

Propping her body up as much as possible, I tied a rope to her wrists, and then connected the ropes in the back of the tree in a tight knot. While she was still out I took the clippers and shaved off sections of her hair, letting them fall in clumps on her lap. Satisfied with my hair cutting skills, I then lit a cigarette and began burning circles on her skin until she woke up.

When she came to, all she could see was a person in a jumpsuit with their face covered. I Krazy-glued her lips together. She struggled in terror as I took cigarette after cigarette out the pack, and burned her with them. After about eight cigarettes, I opened the jar of honey and stood over her, pouring it on top of her head and watching as it ran down the sides of her face and the rest of her body. Once the entire jar was poured out, I began digging holes around her so that any bugs that were in the dirt would come out and feast.

Stepping back to admire my handiwork, I made sure to clear all evidence that would trace this back to me, and I left her there. I changed my clothes back near the fallen tree and stuffed all the evidence in my book bag, then continued my walk through the woods, stopping back at the festival to get a snow cone and cheese pretzel before heading home.

On the news the following morning I could hear Samantha's mom talking to the reporter in a tearful voice because she hadn't come home the night before. They began searching in the woods behind our school where they found her tied to the tree. She had huge black lumps on her skin where the bugs had bitten her, and her wrists were almost cut to the bone from her struggling to get loose.

I laughed to myself as the reporter flashed Ashley, Jessica, and Kevin's case on the news, trying to figure out who was the cause of all the terror that had struck Parkway High School that year. I snickered as I turned over and went back to sleep, enjoying the first day of my summer vacation.

*   *   *

I woke up later in a hospital room with the tube removed from my throat. Although the pain was still there, it wasn't as bad as the effects of the drugs they kept pumping in my system. My uncle was no longer there, but his girlfriend was asleep in the chair next to my bed. I have to honestly say that I didn't like her very much in the beginning, but she had definitely looked out for me since she'd been in the picture. I closed my eyes and rested. When I got out I would take advantage of the rest of my summer because school would be starting in just another month, and I still had some planning to do.

Tanya C. Walker

I must say that I was pleasantly surprised at how Monica had hooked me up when I got home. I was thankful, but she owed it to me. I spent years in the joint fighting bitches off me while she lived the good life, and after one visit I was free to go? It was like I got a get-out-of-jail-free card or something. That just made me wonder if she was really trying to leave me for dead all that time.

Now, I know I was stupid for taking the rap, but at the moment I couldn't think straight. She killed my husband right in front of me, and had no remorse as she popped cap after cap into his face. Marcus was abusive, but damn. I didn't think it would go down like that, so I took the rap, not knowing I would do that much time.

I spent almost four years locked up, but I must say she laced me pretty lovely when I was released. A brand new house, car, and my own restaurant were just a few of the trinkets I received. We had yet to talk, but I couldn't help but hate her. Yeah, she had hooked me up, but she was fucking up too many lives, and when Shaneka told me about the whole Rico thing I almost lost it.

Monica just didn't get it. My new love, Shaneka, had it in for her ass, too. She promised me she would get Monica back, and when she did, I couldn't wait to see the look on her face. When bricks started falling, the building would eventually fall down, and I couldn't wait to see it tumble on her ass. She'd be just like the Wicked Witch from the Wizard of Oz with her damn feet sticking out from under the building, and I'd be right there to take those ruby slippers the hell off.

Jasmine

Curiosity Killed the Cat

I waited until about two weeks after Monica came to my house to go visit her. Even though she had caused all kinds of problems in my life, I needed to know if I still had feelings for her. Call me crazy, but my heart still kind of went out for her.

Things at home were still on shaky ground, but the babies and I were finally settled, and they were happy. James and I had had sex numerous times, but I couldn't get Monica off my mind. Pretending it was her on top of me instead of James was the only way I could cum. Sad, but true.

Being back at work from my three month leave of absence gave me plenty of work to do, but I couldn't concentrate on any of it. My life had changed so much in the last couple of months. For a while I didn't know whether I was coming or going.

All morning I had been trying to get my files in order. I stayed locked in my office because every time I walked past Sheila's old desk I wanted to scream. Why would she do that to me? I mean, no, we weren't the best of friends, but I thought we at least had mutual respect for each other. It was crazy how it all went down, but something was telling me that Sheila really didn't have a choice in the matter. I heard she was working for Judge Stenton now. Maybe I'd pay her a visit, too.

After looking at the clock for the thousandth time I decided it was time I took a lunch break. The senior partners had been absolutely wonderful to me by making sure I had fresh fruit and plenty to drink for the babies, but I needed to get out and get some fresh air. I stopped to let Trish, my new assistant, know I would be taking an extended lunch. I put on my jacket and left with all intentions of getting something to eat and checking on the kids.

On my car ride over to the school I found myself going in the direction of Monica's house. I had planned to just stop and say what was on my mind because I was still pissed about the entire episode that happened at the house. I also wanted to know just what she knew about me fucking the twins, but when she opened the door all of that went out the window.

Monica answered the door in a white wife-beater and pink cotton shorts that barely covered her ass. She had specks of paint on her clothes and skin, and her hair was pulled back into a sloppy ponytail. Her skin glowed and my clit jumped when my eyes made contact with her hard nipples. My mouth watered a little as I remembered how she tasted. Her belly appeared bigger than it was the last time I saw her, and it made her look even more radiant. Guys always said that pregnant pussy was the best pussy, and I was hoping that I would find out if that was true.

We stared at each other without saying any words. I had to keep repeating in my head that she was pregnant by my husband, but it damn sure wasn't working. Maybe if I just tasted her one more time . . .

"Hello, Jasmine. To what do I owe the pleasure of this visit?"

Monica flirted openly from the doorway, and for the first time I noticed her holding a paintbrush as I averted my eyes away from her face. I had to keep a cool head about this.

"I just stopped by to talk to you and see how you were holding up. Do you mind if I come in?"

"No, not at all. I was just about to make something to eat. Would you care for some?"

"Sure."

I followed Monica into the house and into the kitchen after she hung up my jacket. Whatever she was in the midst of making smelled delicious, and as I made myself comfortable, she placed a bowl of beef stew and a tuna sandwich in front of me. I wasted no time digging in.

We ate in silence, looking at each other periodically. I guess neither one of us could believe we were here like this. I think had we not been pregnant, we'd surely be locking ass because I'd be trying to rip her damn head off her shoulders, but today I had come in peace.

"Listen, I was upstairs painting. Care to join me?"

"Sure."

I followed her up the steps, glancing at the photos on the wall on the way up. I thought I recognized James in one of them, but I wasn't sure. I made a mental note to look again on my way down. I stood at the door as she took her seat, the memories flooding my mind at a rapid pace as if they had happened yesterday. Not too long ago I posed for pictures in this very room. Now it looked totally different.

Where there were stacks of paintings, easels, and camera's, now only housed drop cloths, cans of paint, and brushes. The once white walls were now mint green with yellow borders, and Monica was in the middle of creating a mural.

On one wall painted in a blue sky there were doves with ribbons floating from their beaks. There were also babies floating on clouds with wide smiles as angels tickled their feet.

On another wall, she was painting Noah's Ark. I could see some of the animals fully painted and just the outline of others. The room was beautiful, and I had to blink to keep tears from dropping.

"Do you want a change of clothes so you can come in?"

"Huh?" I was so lost in the mural I didn't hear her say anything at first.

"I said, do you want to change your clothes so you won't get paint on your suit?"

"Sure, that sounds perfect."

When she opened her bedroom door I moved straight toward the bed. It was almost like there was a magnetic force pulling me over to it. The pleasure I had received on top of these sheets was unbelievable. I wanted to lay on them one more time, and . . .

"Monica, can I use your phone?"

"It's by the bed."

I called Trish at the job and told her something I ate upset my stomach so I'd be in the next day. She wished me well, and that was that. I set Monica's alarm clock for four thirty so I'd be up to get the kids from daycare. While Monica was in the closet I took my clothes off and stretched out on the soft comforter. It was now one o'clock, so I had some time.

I kept telling myself that I just needed to know if I felt anything for her, but I already knew I did. When she came out of her walk-in closet, she dropped the clothes on the floor, surprised at what she saw.

"Jasmine, I was just . . ."

"Come here. Let me show you how much I missed you."

She was hesitant at first, but I gave her a reassuring look as she began to undress and make her way to the bed. I allowed her to lie on her back and spread her legs.

Taking one of the chocolate pieces from the table next to her bed, I had a brief flashback of the ice sculptures that sat there on my first encounter with Monica. Looking back at

Monica, I got into a comfortable position between her legs. Opening her lips with my thumb and index finger, I rubbed the chocolate against her clit, the candy melting on her hot skin, making her clit look like a chocolate-covered cherry.

Taking my journey a little farther, I took the candy and circled the outside of her opening, licking it all off and starting over again until all the chocolate was gone. Monica moaned and gyrated her hips against my tongue until she came, depositing her honey on my face. I didn't care. I kept her clit trapped between my lips until her shaking subsided.

Kissing a trail up her body, I made sure to pay special attention to her protruding belly, no longer mad that it may have been my husband's child. I decided we would cross that bridge later as I moved to her side and pushed her nipples together, blessing them with my mouth. As soon as I touched her with my tongue, rain began to hit the window panes.

I let Monica touch my clit and finger my pussy with the same rhythm my fingers pleasured her with until we both erupted at the same time. Damn, it'd been a long time since I felt like this, and I wanted it more often.

We fell asleep in each other's arms after I licked her tears away, accepting her apologies and apologizing for the bruise James had left on her beautiful face. We woke up at four, giving us time to have fun in the shower, and giving me time to get dressed.

Before we went downstairs, Monica showed me the middle room, which she'd made into her studio, and a few pictures of the baby furniture she would be ordering. We sat at the table for a second just staring at each other as I waited for the rain to subside.

"Before you go, I have something for you." Monica got up and gave me a box that she had stored in her kitchen. It was light in weight. I was skeptical.

"It's not a bomb, is it?" I said while shaking the box playfully, but serious at the same time.

"No, but you can't open it until you get home." She giggled.

"OK, I can live with that. Now let me go get the kids and get home before James gets there."

"OK."

When we got to the door, I put my jacket on and grabbed the box from her. She looked like she was about to cry. After giving her a hug and promising to call her, I ran to my car, trying to dodge as many raindrops as possible.

When I pulled up to the school I opened the box out of curiosity, and was shocked by what I saw. Pulling them out one at a time, I counted thirteen pairs of underwear, belonging to both me and James. Damn, I guess we were both over there an equal amount of times after all. I decided I wouldn't say anything to James. I'd just put them in the dirty clothes before I started dinner. It didn't make sense to cause any more problems.

When I walked in the house James was already there, and he had started dinner. The kids ran upstairs to wash their hands and change their clothes so I could help them with their homework before dinner. Jalil ran right to James for a hug, but Jaden made a beeline for the steps. I pretended I didn't notice. I left the box in the car when I saw James's car in the driveway. I didn't want to answer any questions, and he'd surely have some once he saw the contents.

I sat down at the table, kicked off my shoes, and waited for the kids to come back down. James walked over to me and tried to kiss me, but I faked a cough before he got too close. I had since washed my face and brushed my teeth at Monica's house, but I didn't want him to get too close and possibly smell her on my skin.

"How was your day, sweetie?" James asked as he stirred the contents of the numerous pots and pans he had on the stove. He looked good in his dress slacks and button-down shirt, but I barely noticed because I had Monica and our afternoon together on my mind.

"It was OK. I just tried to catch up on some work."

"Are you sure? I called your office to check on you and the babies, and your secretary said you left early with an upset stomach."

I was stunned to silence for a split second because I wasn't expecting him to come at me with that. I didn't factor that into the decision to leave early. I shook it off and came back with a lame excuse.

"Yeah, I went to Grandma's Kitchen for lunch, and I think the greens were a bit much. I went to my brother's house to lie down for a while because it was closer from there to get the kids than coming all the way home."

OK, so I told a boldfaced lie, but so what? He'd been lying to me for months. Plus, I knew he'd never call my brother to confirm my stay, but I'd be sure to call and give them a heads up just in case.

"How are you feeling now?"

Before I had a chance to answer, the kids came running into the room, saving me from having to lie again. I immediately began helping them with their homework, thoughts of my afternoon with Monica heavy on my mind. I decided I would continue to see her, but James could never know. I wouldn't see her as much as I used to, but I would still see her.

James set the table after the kids were done with their homework. He served all of us before he sat down. We all lowered our heads to say grace, looking like a fake-ass happy family. I didn't know how all of this was going to end, but I was sure the outcome wouldn't be good.

I listened as my husband and kids conversed. After our meal was done and we had dessert, I bathed the kids and put them to bed. I took a shower and put on a pair of comfy pajamas before getting into bed. Normally, I would have put on something sexy, but I didn't feel like pretending tonight.

I wanted to go to sleep with the feel of Monica's touch on my skin.

Not long after I got in bed, James joined me after taking his shower. I lay in his arms and he rubbed my belly until I went to sleep. My last thought before I submitted to slumber was to remember to get that box out of the trunk of my car. It was his turn to take the kids to school, so I'd have time to go out there and get it after he left in the morning.

James

The Saga Continues

Since all of this craziness had been going on, I'd been trying my damnedest to keep Jazz happy. Lately, Monica had been on my mind a lot, and I badly wanted to grip her by her damn neck. We had an understanding from the beginning. I would let her have sex with my wife once, and that would cover any charges for three sessions. That was the entire reason for setting up the damn threesome, but come to find out they were getting it on like crazy. Jazz had already told me they were, but it didn't hit home until I heard it from Monica's mouth. I'd been looking at Jasmine sideways ever since.

I don't know what came over me when I hit Monica. I guess I was just so mad I couldn't help myself. Jazz pissed me off too, asking Monica questions when I had already told her what I wanted her to know. That conversation was supposed to be over, and there she went bringing up old shit. If we were ever going to move past all of this, then we needed to let it the fuck go. Why keep talking about shit we couldn't change?

Then Jazz jumped on me like I did something wrong—

like she was taking Monica's side. Now, don't get me wrong, I ain't no woman-beater or no shit like that. My father brought me up to have the utmost respect for women, but that bitch was running her mouth and saying shit she had no business speaking out loud. OK, she was pregnant, but I didn't hit her in her stomach, did I? Hell, her face wasn't pregnant.

After that Jazz started acting all funny and shit, and when I called her at work to check on her, Trish said she had already left for the day because she wasn't feeling well. I called her brother's house and her cell phone, but no Jazz. She said she went to her brother's before she got the kids. I guess she got there after I called. I didn't bother to call and confirm because they were family, and I knew he'd just go with the flow. But something wasn't right. I could sense it. I had been trying my hardest to remember what that comment was that Monica had mentioned about some personal trainers for Jazz. I didn't know what that was about because Jazz didn't have any personal trainers that I knew about, but Monica was trying to hint at something. I don't know, maybe Jazz is going to the gym and she doesn't want to tell me. I don't know.

After I called Jazz at the office that day I drove past Monica's house. I thought I saw her car parked on Monica's block, but I knew that it couldn't have been and I made up my mind to ignore it. And if she was indeed there I'm sure it was for a good reason. She seemed a little uneasy when she came in, but I just let it go. If I was going to forgive her, there was no need to keep reliving the past. The trust had to start somewhere.

My morning had been a hectic mess. I wasn't at my desk for five minutes before my day started going wrong. I spilled scalding hot coffee on my shirt as soon as I walked in the office. Not only did I mess up my shirt, but the coffee spilled all over my presentation for a new client. My meeting was at eleven o'clock, so I had to run over to Today's Man to get another shirt before the meeting started. Since I was over the limit on my credit card, I had to purchase the shirt with cash.

Earlier I had told my assistant to have the projector set up and the outline of the presentation in front of every chair in the meeting room. When I walked in, nothing was done. Some days my job is a cake walk. Then there are days like this that make me want to jump off a damn bridge. It took forever to get the slide show set up, and if my luck wasn't bad enough, the copier went down so I had no papers to pass out. It was a wonder Nabisco signed the contract at all. I kept assuring them that we were normally more organized, and that their account was in good hands.

The Urban News Network would be shooting a commercial for a new line of fat free cookies they would be selling in the near future. My thing was, if you were supposed to be on a diet, why the hell were you eating cookies? Women—can't live with them, can't afford them after the breakup.

After barely getting through my morning, I called my wife to see if she wanted to hook up for lunch. It'd been a little tense at home for the last two weeks, so I figured this would be a good icebreaker. A man could only go for so long without getting his dick wet, and I was lying next to some ass every night, yet lately I couldn't seem to get none. Something had to give, and soon. I wouldn't step out on her again though. I'd learned my lesson from the shit I was going through with Monica, and how I almost got busted with those strippers, so I was cool on that note, but what was I supposed to do?

When I called her office the first time, her secretary said she was in a meeting, so I opted to call back as opposed to leaving her a message. I wanted to talk to her personally. A half hour later I was connected to her, but she sounded like she had an attitude. I had my own shit going on, and I didn't feel like all that, but I guess she was having a bad day too.

"Hey, sweetheart, how's your day going?" I asked extra

cheerfully, trying to change her mood. Both of us didn't need to be angry at the world.

"I've had better mornings. What's up with you?"

"Nothing. I had a little time to spare so I was hoping we could meet up for a quick lunch. Maybe check out that new soul food spot that just opened up in University City."

"Which one? Tondalayah's?"

"Yeah, that's the spot. I heard the food is banging, and the iced tea is off the chain."

"Your treat?"

"Of course."

"I'm game."

"Cool. I'll meet you outside your job at one thirty. Tell Trish you're taking an extended lunch. I just landed the account with Nabisco, so we have a reason to celebrate."

After hanging up with her, I went to talk to my boss for a few, and he gave me the rest of the day off for pulling off getting the account in spite of the disasters from this morning. I made sure to call P.B.S.I., the temporary agency I worked with, so they could send me another assistant, and dismiss the one who was here. This was a major corporation, and we were making moves. I didn't have time for what had happened earlier. If everything were set up earlier, I wouldn't have had most of my morning problems to begin with.

I straightened up my desk, took one last look at the photo of me, Jazz, and the kids, left the office, and made my way across town to meet my wife for lunch. Hopefully the rest of my day would go smoother.

Sheila

Old Flames

Early Monday morning, I was waiting outside the hospital for Monica. Initially she told me the class started at four, but she called me back yesterday to let me know she would be taking the ten a.m. class instead. She pulled up ten minutes late in a cute, hot pink jumpsuit, her belly a bulge at the bottom. I said nothing to her as she took her time getting out the car and passing the valet her keys as if she wasn't already late.

All of the memories from the previous year flooded my mind as we took a quiet elevator ride up to the tenth floor of the building. Monica still looked the same, yet different. I could still see her devil's horns, but her eyes looked like those of a scared child. I was sympathetic, but determined not to get caught up in her shit this time. Hell, she was carrying a married man's child, and I wanted no part of the fiasco. If I was going to hell I'd like it to be for some shit I did, not because of someone else's.

I was almost positive it was James's baby, but with Monica, you just never knew. I still needed to talk to my sister about the shit that went down with her husband, Hill, and Monica, but I hadn't found the time or the nerve. Hill was a cool dude and all, but there was always something sneaky about him that I didn't particularly care for. Now I knew why.

During the class, I helped Monica learn her breathing exercises, but I wasn't committing anything to memory because I would not be there to help her deliver. Lamaze class was one thing, but childbirth was another. We went through the motions of counting breathing repetitions, but on the real, all of that shit went out the window when it came time to push. That was the number one reason why I only had one child. The shit hurt like hell. I guarantee if men had to carry children and give birth, we'd be an endangered species.

After class, Monica invited me to brunch at Tondalayah's, a new soul food restaurant that opened up a while back in University City. I kept planning in my mind to get down there, but I never got around to it. I was really ready to go home and chill since Monica fixed it so I had a paid day off.

"Sure, I'll go, but you're driving."

During the ride over my heart was beating a mile a minute. It'd been a long time since I'd been this close to Monica, and I wasn't sure if I liked the feelings I was having. She turned my life completely upside down in less than a year, but my pussy was throbbing like everything was cool between us. I kept telling myself not to fall for her, but my body was betraying me. Just thinking about the things her mouth could do had me spent.

We chatted about various things on the way over, avoiding the obvious. I damn sure wasn't going to be the one to bring it up. My sister warned me this morning about helping her, but I was just trying to pay my debt so I could move on. She cursed me something horrible when I told her where I was going.

"You're doing what? Ain't that the bitch who had you caught up in that married couple's shit just a few months ago?" She was hot with me, and spared no feelings or expletives as she took my son out my arms and began removing his jacket from his body. My sister was ready to beat Monica's ass not too long ago, so I understood her anger, but I was not in the mood to explain. I mean, I had a good job at the law firm. Yes, I have a better job now, but Monica put me through so much stress in the past that the fact we even talk is a miracle.

"Yeah, but I owe her, Tiffany. Yeah, she had me in some crazy shit, but if it weren't for her I wouldn't have gotten the job down at the courthouse. She made it possible for me to provide for Devon."

"No, bitch, your job skills made it possible to provide for your son. She's fucking the judge. That's how she got close to him. She's a fuckin' slut. Ho Rider number one and shit, and ya ass is about to be following close behind her."

"Tiff, it ain't that serious."

"It is that serious, Sheila. Ain't this bitch killin' people and shit? You go right on ahead, but don't dial my number when the block is hot. If anything happens to my nephew, that's your ass. Don't take it as a threat, because that ass whipping is promised. Put ya check on it."

My sister's words echoed in my head non-stop, but I figured Monica had to have calmed down at least a little bit now that she was pregnant. Her stomach was definitely showing her pregnancy, so I didn't think she'd be making too much noise, but then again, with Monica you never knew.

We pulled up to the restaurant twenty minutes later, and the smells from the kitchen had my mouth watering. I had neglected breakfast because I was in a rush to meet Monica and get it over with, but the growling noise in my stomach gave away my hunger to everyone in the place.

Tondalayah's was a nice spot. The whole place looked inviting, even from the outside. There were about ten tables in the dining area, and the entire restaurant was candlelit. On the walls there were black and white photos of great music legends from the past and present, including a poster-sized picture of Aja and Fatin, the voices behind the talented Kindred the Family Soul.

The walls were mauve with a fuchsia, hunter green, and

white floral border around the top. The candleholders were made of mauve and hunter green crystal resting on top of gold plates to hold the tea light candles. The wait staff was extremely friendly—the women dressed in black tops and skirts, and the men in black shirts and slacks. I just loved the ambiance in the place. After seating us and filling our glasses with mixed fruit iced tea, the waitress took our order and we were served hot, buttered biscuits.

At first we looked around the restaurant, avoiding eye contact. I glanced her way a few times when she wasn't looking, and I had to say that pregnancy brought out the best in her. She appeared to be glowing from the inside out, and it looked like her hair had grown a lot in the last couple of months. My coochie was talking to me again, but I wasn't having it. After the James and Jasmine drama, I knew I could never get that deep in someone else's issues again.

Before the moment could get any more awkward, our food was served and we began eating. She talked a little about a mural she was painting in what would be the baby's room, and invited me to come see it. I just looked at her like she was crazy. I didn't give a damn if Noah was building a new ark on top of her house and we had to go there to avoid the flood. I'd be a drowned bitch before I stepped into that house again. Ain't no way I was going over there, come hell or high water.

Our conversation was improving, and we were really enjoying ourselves until Monica practically jumped out of her seat, sprinted across the restaurant, and ended up in another woman's arms. Was I jealous? Not really, but when I saw her reaction I felt something. They exchanged words, and a few minutes later they started walking toward the table. The woman looked familiar, but I couldn't remember where I had seen her face. Monica was all smiles like she had just hit the damn Powerball. I mustered up a weak smile as they got closer to the table, but I was feeling sick to my stomach at the sight before me.

"Sheila, this is Tanya Walker, a good friend of mine. Tanya, this is Sheila, one of my many associates."

My face almost cracked and fell on the floor at Monica's introduction, but I got my shit together real quick and reached out to shake Tanya's hand. Her face frowned up a little when Monica said they were friends, but I let it pass, not really knowing the meaning behind it.

"Nice to meet you, Tanya."

"Thank you so much. I hope you're enjoying your meal."

"Oh, I am. It's delicious."

Monica rudely pulled Tanya to the side and they continued to converse while I attempted to finish my meal. Not sure what made me glance out the window, I nearly spit my food across the table when I saw James helping Jasmine out the car. I crossed my fingers and tried to cross my toes, hoping to every god on the planet that they were not coming here. All hope went out the door when James opened it and the couple walked inside.

I watched Monica's face for a reaction. At that same moment Tanya walked away. It then hit me where I knew Tanya from. I remembered seeing her face on the front of the newspaper when all that shit went down with her husband being killed. I couldn't really remember the story at that second, but I made a mental note to research it when I got home.

In the meantime, Monica, Jazz, and James were stuck on stupid, standing there staring at each other. I got up to go to the bathroom in an effort to avoid any unnecessary chaos. On my way to the back of the restaurant I was stopped by Tanya in the walkway by the kitchen.

"Let me talk to you for a second."

I said nothing. I just followed her into the storage room so we could talk. I was nervous because I didn't know what she was going to do. I didn't remember seeing Monica's name in the article, but I was assuming they were once lovers.

"How long have you known Monica?" she asked as if she had a big secret.

"About a year or so. Why?"

"Honey, you are walking around with trouble, you hear me? Run while you can."

For some reason I trusted Tanya at the moment, and figured if we both put our heads together maybe we could get Monica's ass back. I wasn't sure what role Monica played in Tanya having to serve time, but I was sure it was all her fault. I'd also been sitting on the tape I'd taken from Monica's for a couple of months, and I needed to share what I knew with someone. Maybe she could help me out.

"Listen, is there a way we could meet up after business hours? I have a feeling we need to talk," I said.

"Here's my home, cell, and restaurant number. Contact me as soon as you can. This is serious." Tanya scribbled her info on the top page of her receipt book. I folded the paper and stuck it in my back pocket, careful to stick it all the way down so I wouldn't lose the number. Some serious shit was about to pop off. I could feel it.

I pretended I was drying my hands on my jeans when I walked out to the front. Jazz and James were seated at a table, and Monica was standing by the door waiting for me. Our food had been put into carryout containers, and our tea in sports bottles. I was hesitant to walk past Jazz and James, but I had no choice. It was the only way out the restaurant.

As I walked, I kept my eyes on Monica, avoiding eye contact with Jazz and James. I was going to walk by without a word, but I couldn't. In my mind I felt I owed Jasmine an apology, and now would be the perfect time, just in case the opportunity never presented itself again.

"Jasmine, I don't want to interrupt your meal, but I just have one thing to say." I was an emotional mess at this point. I literally had to blink back tears as I stared into Jasmine's angry face. I knew I had to make amends somehow.

Jasmine's entire face scrunched up like she had smelled something foul. Monica, I'm sure, was boring a damn hole in the side of my head, but I had to get it out. James just sat there and looked straight ahead, his hands tensing up into tight fists on the tabletop.

"Sheila, what can you say? The damage is done."

"I know, and I just wanted you to know that I never meant to hurt you. I'm sorry for all the confusion I caused."

"Listen," James said abruptly. His eyes appeared to be shooting red flames, and it was clear he was trying to keep his composure. "My wife is pregnant and doesn't need any extra stress. What's done is done. Let's not keep reliving the past."

My mouth dropped. I was at a complete loss for words. Jasmine was pregnant? Who would've guessed that? I turned to see the look on Monica's face, but all I heard was the chime on the door as I saw her wobble quickly across the street. I apologized once more and rushed out the door, barely making it to Monica's car.

Monica said nothing the entire ride, and I offered her no condolences. All I could do was hope that Jazz would hear me out one day. I knew I should let it go, but I just couldn't. I was indecisive about what I would do to get back at Monica, but I knew once I got a chance to talk to Tanya everything would be cool.

Monica dropped me off at my car in a huff, barely letting me get out of the car and close the door before she pulled off. I had a plan forming in my head, and I couldn't wait to get back to the restaurant. I had to beg my sister to watch my son a little while longer. Finally, she agreed to an extra hundred dollars and a platter from Tondalayah's as payment for watching my son.

Before I left the house I grabbed the tape I took from Monica's, stuffed it in my bag, and made a beeline to the other side of town. I had some business to take care of that couldn't wait until the end of the day.

Sheila

Stolen Secrets

I pulled up to the restaurant about an hour later, my heart beating wildly. I had to count to ten and get my head together before I could get out of my car. Some serious shit was about to go down, and I had to be on point if it was going to go down right. When I walked into the restaurant James and Jazz were gone. That alleviated some of the stress. Tanya saw me when I walked in. I took a seat at the closest table before I ended up stretched out on the floor from an anxiety attack.

"Tanya," I said to her between breaths. I was really trying to keep my composure but it was killing me. "I know you said to come after closing hours, but I couldn't wait that long. Is there a way we can go now somewhere to talk? I don't think I can make it until the end of the day."

"Sure. I was just saying to my mate that I couldn't wait that long either. Let me just get my stuff from the back and we can roll out. Smitty can handle everything here for the rest of the day."

I sat there attempting to get my head straight. I noticed that Tanya said her 'mate,' and I was curious to see if it would be another woman. A few minutes later she walked out with a beautiful woman next to her.

This woman resembled Monica in so many ways it was scary. They had similar looks, and although their faces weren't exactly the same, they could have easily been cousins. Her style of dress and the way she wore her hair was nearly identical to Monica's. If I hadn't just left Monica not too long ago, you couldn't have told me she wasn't standing before me. The only thing missing was the pregnant belly.

"Sheila, this is my soul mate, Shaneka. Baby, this is Sheila, the woman I told you about earlier."

"Nice to meet you," we said in unison, causing a slight smile to spread across our faces. That definitely relieved some of the tension between us. I was grateful. For the first time I felt like I was doing the right thing, and I couldn't wait to get started.

"Tanya, I'll follow you guys. I hope you have a VCR at your house. We'll need it."

The three of us left the restaurant and hastily went to my car. I couldn't wait to get this shit out in the open . . . finally. A half hour later we pulled up to a beautiful house in Wyncote, a suburb of Philly. The neighborhood was so quiet I felt that if I breathed too loudly everyone would hear me. We got out of the car and headed toward a stunning peach and cream house that sat so far back off the street you had to drive up to get to the door.

"Tanya, your house is beautiful," I exclaimed. I had never in my life seen a community so tranquil. This could definitely be a place to raise my son.

"Thanks to Monica. It was her hard-earned money that paid for it."

Something told me there was more behind that statement, but I didn't question it. I knew we were about to get into some heavy shit and all would be discussed in a matter of time.

The inside of her home was just as impeccable as the outside. Tasteful furnishings peppered the sunken-in living room, and several pieces of art adorned the buttercream walls. The paintings I guessed were gifts from Monica because I recognized her in a few of them.

We went straight to the back of the house and down a few steps to an entertainment room. There was a television the size of my damn apartment in there, and every gadget you could think of. Shaneka pushed a button, and an entire wall moved to the side and revealed a beautiful entertainment system. She pushed a few more buttons, and the VCR came from behind a shelf and positioned itself in front of the television, ready to accept the tape. I dug through my bag and nervously gave the tape to Shaneka. She and Tanya sat on the couch. I sat in the chair.

You could cut the tension in the room with a knife as we patiently waited for the tape to rewind and start. I took one last deep breath as I watched the tape begin to play.

I had never watched the tape, besides the parts that Monica had shown me, and I had no idea what I had missed. The tape opened with James and Monica in what appeared to be a hotel room. She had him blindfolded and tied to the bed, his dick standing straight up in the air like a thick, black pole. She rode him in positions I didn't even know were possible. I found myself getting a little turned on by their actions, but I quickly checked myself. That wasn't what I was there for.

The first segment of the tape ended with Monica balancing her hands on his stomach, and stretching her legs out like a gymnast would on a balance beam. She then proceeded to push her body up and down with her arms, riding his dick until his ejaculation slid down the sides of his dick. The camera was zoomed in so close you could see his dick pulsate as his seed spilled from the head and into Monica's eagerly awaiting womanhood. I was amazed at her skill.

A scene with her, Jazz, and James followed. James was leaning against a dresser in a different hotel room stroking his
dick while Monica and Jazz performed on the bed. Jazz
looked a little hesitant at first, but after some coaching, she
got into it. As the tape played I went from being amazed, to
being upset, to not believing what the hell I was watching.

She had the mayor of Washington, DC in all kinds of compromising positions. That shit turned the hell out of my
stomach, because he was a fat, nasty bastard with a big bul-
bous nose, and even bigger body cavity. He reminded me a
lot of the character Fat Bastard from that Austin Powers movie.
Still, she was all over him like he was Denzel Washington. I had
to turn my head from the television when she began stroking
his ass with a strap-on dildo like he was the woman and she
was the man. Tanya and Shaneka just sat there with their
mouths wide open, not knowing what to say.

A couple of scenes went by with people I didn't recognize,
and a few more of Jazz and James. My sister's husband, Hill,
popped up with a quick episode by the fireplace and a few
other guys from the police force who I recognized from last
year's Christmas party were acting a fool on camera too.
Monica must have a camera set up in every room of her
house. I just sat there in awe, not believing what I saw.

I almost lost my lunch when I saw Monica and Stenton on
the tape. She had him handcuffed to the bed in the doggy-
style position, blind folded, and dressed in a maid's outfit
giving it to him from the back. I had to close my eyes and
cover my ears so I wouldn't be able to hear the sounds from
the television. I couldn't believe I saw my boss in a position
like that, and all the women that come and go from his office is shocking.

After the tape was done, Shaneka got up and started pushing buttons on one of the many remotes that lay on the front
case of the entertainment center. After about five minutes,
two tapes popped out. She gave me one, and labeled the

other before putting it away in a drawer by the bookcase. I knew at that moment that she had made a copy for herself, and I briefly wondered if I had done the right thing.

I waited for them to get situated, because that was truly a lot to take in at one time. We sat in silence for what felt like an eternity. I briefly flashed through my life over the past five years wondering why I always ended up in situations like this. The sound of Tanya's voice interrupted my trip down memory lane as I came back to deal with the situation at hand.

"Sheila, I just want to thank you for stepping forward with this matter. Knowing how Monica is, that took a lot of courage on your part, and I want you to know that as of this moment you have no need to fear her again. Trust me on that."

"I want to get my life back. I can't live like this, constantly looking over my shoulders, wondering if she's going to jump out of the damn bushes on me."

"Listen, when I first met Monica I fell for the bullshit, too. She was sexing me crazy and had me thinking that we could truly be together. Even after she killed my husband I knew she would be there for me, but she never came."

Tanya went on to tell me how her husband, Marcus, had been a loving and devoted man to her and her son. He was an excellent father and a wonderful provider, but when he got drunk, another side of him presented itself. He became extra abusive, even putting her in the hospital with broken bones on a couple of occasions. He was the provider, and she was the caregiver, so she stayed home to raise their son, although she always had dreams of opening her own restaurant. Marcus had promised to one day let her have her own business.

Monica became impatient, not letting Tanya handle the breakup her way. On the night Tanya was supposed to leave Marcus, he had been out drinking. The situation turned violent when he saw Tanya and their son's stuff packed by the door. Tanya had told Monica she would drive over to her house, but Monica took it upon herself to come and get Tanya. Monica walked in at the moment when Marcus was about to hit Tanya again. Monica tried to protect Tanya, and when Marcus turned to swing at her she pulled a gun out and unloaded it into his face. Monica fled the scene, promising Tanya she wouldn't have to do any time if she took the rap. And like a fool, Tanya copped to the murder, spending a little over three years in jail.

"She looked possessed when she was pulling the trigger. Like she went back in time to another point in her life or something," Tanya said with a spaced-out look on her face.

We all talked for a little while, and then Shaneka brought it all together so it made sense. We had to get Monica back, but we would wait for the baby to be born. That way, we wouldn't be imprisoned for harming a fetus and we could just handle our shit and not have to worry about an unborn child.

"That sounds like a good plan, Shaneka, but what do we do right now?"

"Now we go to see James and Jasmine. They need to know what kind of shit they were pulled into. Revenge should be sweet, and I'm sure they'd want a piece of it too."

"Are you sure that's a good idea? I honestly think all they want is to move on and put their lives back together. I don't think they would want in on it." I tried to persuade them to think otherwise, simply because I wasn't ready to face Jazz and James again, but it was apparent they weren't trying to hear that.

"Let's at least show them the tape," Shaneka argued back. It wasn't until she told me about her beef with Monica and Rico that I understood what she was trying to do.

"OK, you guys can follow behind me. We might as well go and get it over with."

During the drive over I tried to envision how it would all go down. I mean, I was a lover, not a fighter, and I didn't know if Jasmine could take seeing me twice in one day. I was on that tape giving her husband head. I didn't exactly sleep with him, but that was damn close. I knew if it was me, I'd be ready to go on a head-smashing spree. On the flip side, I think she needed to know. James was wrong, there was no doubt about that, but even Jazz knew how persuasive Monica could be.

When we got there I let Tanya ring the bell. If Jazz was going to swing, I didn't want it to be on me. I knew she was going through a tough time, especially being pregnant. What were they going to do with another kid, and with Monica possibly carrying James's child? I didn't want to be there when that shit went down. When Jazz opened the door her face let us know she didn't feel like the nonsense. I stayed in the back behind Shaneka while Tanya explained our reason for being there.

"What tape are you talking about? Where did you get it from?" Jasmine had yet to open the door fully. I didn't see James's car, so I figured she would be apprehensive about letting us inside because she was home alone, but the last thing I would allow was for her to come to any harm.

"I took it from Monica's house the night she was taken to the hospital for a miscarriage," I explained to Jazz. "I just wanted to have some proof of what she was doing."

Jazz looked at us like we were crazy, but she eventually let us in. The place looked different. I didn't know how I would react to seeing her again, but I was glad she gave us this time to talk. Once we were all seated, I mustered up enough courage to finally say something to her.

"Jazz, I know you don't necessarily want to hear anything I have to tell you, but after you watch this tape, maybe we can discuss some things."

"Sheila, you know you hurt me the most. I understand that we weren't close, but damn, you set me up in the worst way, and in my eyes that's unforgivable."

"It wasn't even my idea. I was trying to talk Monica out of it. She wouldn't hear anything I had to say."

"That's funny, because she blamed it all on you when she came here."

"Did she? Well, since when could her word be taken as the truth? She's a manipulator. She'll say whatever she needs to say to get you off her back."

"As true as that may be, it doesn't excuse you. You knew what was going down, that's why none of your shit was on your desk when you left for the day. I knew something was up, but I didn't expect to come home to your raggedy ass on my kitchen table."

"Look, we're not here for all that. Y'all can rehash the past once we're gone. I just need you to look at this tape," Tanya explained.

Both of us looked at Tanya like she was crazy. I said nothing after that. Jazz got up, snatched the tape out of my hands, and popped it in the VCR. I just sat back and watched her face as she watched Monica in action. There was going to be some shit when it was over. I could feel it. I knew Tanya, Shaneka, and I were planning to get Monica back once she had her baby, and we planned to discuss how once Jazz finished watching the tape. All hell was about to break loose, and for the first time in my life, I couldn't wait.

Tanya

Playing Catch Up: Through Tanya's Eyes

Seeing Monica on that tape brought back so many memories. At the time we were together I was in love with her, and I couldn't see how mentally sick she was. I, too, was caught up in her web of lies and deceit, and for a brief time in my life I wanted to believe I was in love with her. She presented a stability that I couldn't get at home, and I craved to live life on the other side of the fence. I soon found out that the grass wasn't as green as I thought it was.

I met her at an art demonstration down at CCP (the Community College of Philadelphia) during fashion week. She had a few pieces on display, and I was in awe of the detail displayed in her work. Before I knew the woman in the picture, I was intrigued. Her eyes drew you into the painting, having you believe that she could see into your soul, taking the breath out of your lungs.

I was standing there in a trance staring at a painting of her lying on a chaise lounge the color of fall leaves. The fireplace strategically placed off in the corner of the painting looked lifelike. Her use of colors was impeccable. I must have zoned out because I didn't realize she was standing

next to me until she spoke. Her voice sounded like a rushing
waterfall. I was hooked from day one.

"My living room used to look like that just last year, but I
went with a new color scheme for the New Year."

I turned toward the direction of the voice, surprised to see
her face to face. She looked almost angelic . . . almost. There
was a hint of mystery behind her eyes I couldn't figure out at
the time, but now I know it was nothing but the damn devil.
If I knew then what I know now.

"So, you're the artist? It is truly a pleasure meeting you. I
must tell you that your work is absolutely wonderful. I'll be
purchasing this one for my living room," I said to her while
shaking her hand. The skin of her palm felt like silk, and I
could only imagine how her hands would feel on the rest of
me.

"Thank you so much. I appreciate the patronage." She
blushed, looking away for a brief moment before resuming
eye contact. I smiled to myself and turned my attention back
to the painting on the wall.

"Listen, what are you doing after the demonstration?
There's a café down the street, a few doors away. Maybe we
can chat over an espresso," Monica invited.

"That would be nice. I'll meet you at the entrance when
it's all done."

"That's fine, and don't worry about paying for this painting. I'll be sure that you get it before you go."

"You don't have to do that. This painting costs five thousand dollars. I can't let you pay for that."

"Did you forget I painted it? It wouldn't cost me anything," she replied with a cute laugh that made me follow
suit. I burned her smile into my memory at that moment.

"OK, I'll meet you at the door."

She said nothing. She walked away and began mingling
with the other guests. I made my way to the door to avoid the
crowd that was sure to come. There had to be nothing but

ballers in here, because these painting were a grip, but all of the money made went to The Sanctuary, an organization that extended their hand to teenage girls who had been molested. It was a good cause that brought out plenty of supporters with big bucks. I saw the mayor of D.C. and his family there, as well as a few other bigwigs in political positions, and many members of the police force.

I wasn't waiting long before I saw her making her way through the crowd. We had yet to exchange names, so I couldn't call out to her. I waved my hands in the air until she saw me. Her smile blessed my eyes once again.

"You ready?" she asked as she pushed her way through the door.

"Yep, let's get out of here."

We made light conversation on our way down to the café, and once we got inside we grabbed a table by the door. After our orders were placed, we were finally able to converse, exchanging names before we moved along in line.

She told me all about her life as an artist/photographer, and I actually remembered seeing some of the covers she did for *Essence, Sister2Sister,* and *Vibe* magazines. I wanted to ask her why she started The Sanctuary, but it was obvious she had been hurt coming up so there wasn't any need to go there.

I told her about my job as head chef at The French Quarters, and my dream of one day owning my own restaurant. My husband wouldn't allow me to work after our son was born, and I became a stay-at-home mom, but I didn't think she needed to know all of that. I let her know I was married, choosing to be up front about my status. It was obvious she was trying to get to know me on a personal level. I was open to all the possibilities.

"This is my son, Tyler, and my husband, Marcus." I showed her a picture in my wallet from the days when we were a happy family.

When Marcus and I first got together he knew I was into women, and he was all for it as long as I brought them home so we could share. I figured we could do the same with Monica, but I didn't find out until much later from a friend of mine that Marcus already knew Monica before I did. That was the reason he purchased the ticket to the art demonstration. It was all a setup to get us together on his terms. I was the only one who didn't know about it.

Giving it to her straight, no chaser, I told her what my husband and I were into and that I thought she would be perfect for an evening of adult pleasure. She agreed, but only after I agreed to meet with her one-on-one beforehand. She said she didn't mind sharing me with my husband, but she wanted to see what I was about first. We set a date to meet the next night.

I knew Marcus wouldn't go for that, so I told him I would be out with a few girlfriends and I needed him to watch the baby. Of course he objected, stating that if I got to go out why couldn't he? It wasn't until I told him I'd see about bringing a woman home that he agreed.

I called the number Monica gave me and we set a time. I was to be at her house by eight that night and I was pulling up at seven fifty, eagerly knocking on her door. My breath was taken away upon walking into her house. I loved how she mixed various shades of pink to make up the décor. She later revealed that she furnished, painted, and set up every room in the house herself.

We walked straight upstairs to a gorgeous bedroom. We didn't waste time on formalities or anything like that. I knew why I was there, so we needed to make it happen. This girl could do things with her tongue that you would never believe unless you had a Monica experience yourself. I thought I was Spider-Woman, and it was obvious that Monica thought she was Spider-Woman, too, because every wall I climbed, she climbed up right behind me, never taking her tongue from my clit.

I thought about my husband for all of four seconds before the next wave of orgasms came crashing down and wiped him from my memory. We tossed and turned and climbed all over each other for hours, causing me to miss my curfew.

When I returned home it was obvious that Marcus had been drinking. He staggered into the living room when I opened the front door. An empty Hennessy bottle was on the table. I moved to check on the baby, but he grabbed me by my neck and pinned me against the wall. The smell of his breath made me want to vomit, but I forced it down while trying to catch my breath at the same time.

"You were supposed to be in this house. Where were you, and why did you walk through my door by yourself?"

"I . . . I can't," I attempted to answer him, but the tightening of his fist around my throat made it difficult to breathe and talk at the same time. At the very moment I thought I would black out, he let me go. I fell to the floor on my knees, gasping for air. The room spun around in circles for a while. I barely had time to recover when I saw stars from the impact of his fist connecting fiercely with the side of my face.

"Get on your knees," he demanded, pulling me up by my hair. I obliged, if only to stop the stabbing pain shooting into my head from the grip he had on my roots. I didn't know how much longer I could take this abuse. Something had to give, and soon.

"Marcus, can you please let go of my head? I can't see."

"You don't need to see to suck a dick. Just open your mouth." I had no other choice but to do what he said. He forced his dick into my mouth repeatedly, causing me to gag on several occasions.

I did the best I could for the three minutes it took him to explode. He came so much a good amount of it shot out of my nose, and the rest I either swallowed or spit out. I spent the next minute or so sputtering on the floor trying to catch my breath. He left me there for dead, warning me not to come in late next time, and especially by myself. That was just one of the scenarios that pushed me closer to Monica, and ultimately led to his demise.

I saw Monica a few times after that, and once we had the threesome we started hooking up even more. Of course, Marcus didn't like it, not believing the story I gave him about us just being shopping buddies. He would whip my ass, and she would heal my wounds. This went on for a few months until finally she got tired.

We had decided that my son and I would move in with her and be a family. By this time Marcus had already cracked one of my ribs, tried to slit my wrist, and had pulled a patch of hair out from the side of my head that I now covered with a weave track. They were threatening to fire me from The French Quarters. Between Marcus calling there a million times a day for absolutely nothing, and me missing days from work because I was hiding injuries, it just wasn't working out, and my life was spiraling downhill quickly.

Three more weeks went by and he punched me in my face for not having dinner done, breaking my nose in the process. That night Monica decided I would leave him. I went home to pack my stuff while he was at work, but he came home in the middle of me packing my son's stuff.

We were in the living room arguing back and forth because I was trying to leave. I had more than enough money in my checking account to start over, and decided I would just leave whatever belongings I had there. He wouldn't let me leave, and even after I grabbed my son to keep him from hitting me, he still continued to batter my body with wild blows from his heavy hands. I balled up in the corner to cover my face and the baby, and just when I moved to punch him in his private area, Monica burst in through the front door.

I can't remember what she said to him, all I knew was he moved in her direction to swing at her and she unloaded her gun into his face, afterward reloading and finishing him off. When she was done there was nothing left of his head.

I was devastated. Yes, I wanted him gone, but damn. I was stuck, literally. I couldn't move at first. The cries from my son brought me back to reality. I held his small body close to mine in an effort to quiet him as I stepped closer to my husband's dead body. The tears were uncontrollable as the reality of what happened set in.

"What did you do? Monica, what did you do?" I screamed after I sat the baby down in the crib. I couldn't believe he was gone. Now what would my son do for a father?

"What did I do? Bitch, I took you out of your misery."

"Monica, you just killed a person. Do you know how much time you get for murder?"

"Tanya, you won't be in there long. I have connections who will have you out in no time. Just tell the police it was a break-in that went bad."

"What do you mean *I* won't be in there long? I am not taking the rap for this. Fuck what you heard!" I was back on my feet and ready to beat Monica's ass. I wasn't doing time for anyone, damn the jokes. Who I look like, Boo Boo the Fool?

"Tanya, listen to what I'm saying to you. If I do the time, how can I take care of you? The most you'll spend is a few hours at the precinct for questioning. Call me when you get down there and I'll come get you. OK?"

For some strange reason I believed her, and followed her instructions. I should have known she wasn't shit. When I got down to the precinct and tried to call, she didn't answer her phone. Yeah, she got me a bomb ass lawyer, but I spent damn near four years in the bricks before she came for me. I was in there fighting bitches off, ending up with a damn scar on my face from some of them creeping up on me late at night trying to rape me.

When I got out she laced me, but by then Shaneka told me she had a lot to do with Rico getting axed.

As Shaneka drove us home from Jazz's house that night I let my head rest on the seat while I tried to get my thoughts together. We'd lay low for a while until Monica had her baby. It was only right.

I looked over at Shaneka and watched her as she concentrated on the road. She had held me down from the first day we met, and I wasn't sure I would have made it without her. I owed my very sanity to her, and her patience. She made me complete, and her love was unconditional. She gave me exactly what I thought I got from Monica—love and attention. Monica's day was coming, and soon.

When we pulled up to the house I waited until she opened the door. We held hands as we walked up to the house, and once inside we connected as one in front of the fireplace. She scratched my itch and I scratched hers until the sun rose. Love definitely made things happen.

Carlos

Flash Forward

"**B**ring that nigga in here. It's time to end all of this right now."

Jesus, Hector, and I had set up the block about three months ago to see what Arturo was up to. And now we finally had him where we wanted him. When we met back up that night, I have to say my feelings were hurt to find out that Rico trusted Arturo more than me, even though I was supposed to be his right hand man. I had asked Rico on many occasions to introduce me to his connect, just in case some shit went down, but he never did. Then I found out that this nigga Arturo done been to see him at least five times since Rico was done in.

Jesus and Hector had spent the last hour beating Arturo nearly to death. Killing him wouldn't get me the information I needed, so I had to keep him alive for at least a little while. They brought his bloodied body into the living room, sitting him in one of the kitchen chairs and securing his hands and feet to the arms and legs. Honestly, I don't think Arturo would've taken such a harsh beating had he gone

one-on-one with them. Hector would have been an easy win
for him, but Jesus would have definitely taken his life.

"So, Arturo, what do you have to say for yourself?"

It took him a minute to focus on me. I'm sure the room
was spinning, no doubt from the multiple blows to his head.
I'd decide later if I wanted him around. Dishonor meant
death—no more, no less.

"Listen, Carlos, all I did was what Rico told me to do."

"What did he tell you?"

"He told me to make sure that chick he was fucking with
took care of his shit. I think her name was Monique or Monica
or some shit like that. We went ring shopping and everything for her, man. He was really in love with her, and he was
leaving Shaneka to the birds."

"What did that have to do with his connect? How did you
get to meet him?"

I was trying to put two and two together, but it wasn't making sense. I knew Rico had it bad for Monica from back in the
day, and Shaneka was supposed to take her place, but I didn't
think it was that serious. Yeah, he started to slip a little with
the spending, but I knew Monica kept the jakes off him for a
little while because she had connections. This nigga was riding around town like he was the fucking President of the
United States or something, like his ass was untouchable. But
I knew something had to be going down, so that's why I
started to investigate as soon as shit started looking suspicious.

"Well, one time we went out shopping for a house for
Monica and he told me how it was better to put a safe in her
house and keep the money there, so if the cops ever searched
the apartment they wouldn't find anything. That's how she
got the cash, and all his shit. The day after he got locked up,
she told me to help her move all of the stuff out before the
cops came back, and as payback for helping her she'd take
me to the connect to re-up on the supply."

"So, she knows who the connect is?"

"Yeah, she directed me to the house and waited in the car while I handled business in his mansion. Rico said he couldn't trust you, that's why he never took you over there. He felt you were always trying to stick him."

That hurt like hell to hear those words spoken out loud. Rico and I have been to hell and back. I shot dudes dead for him on more than one occasion. Before all of that we came from grade school together, sharing clothes and barely eating. I loved him like a brother, even though I felt like I needed to take charge, but I would've never brought harm to his doorstep.

"What happened when Rico got to jail?"

Arturo broke it down how once word was out that Rico got knocked, Juan had his boy who was on the same block as Rico set shit up while everyone was at dinner. Rico was sleeping with one of the guards for phone privileges, and he called me to find out what the word was on the street. He had suspicions that Monica had set him up, and I remember vividly the day he called me with his concerns.

* * *

"State ya purpose," I spoke into the phone as I made my way down the avenue. The block had been hot since the day Rico was got, and they were sweeping niggas up off the street left and right. Three of my boys had gone down, and all I could do was wait to see who started singing. Time would definitely make a man confess. Believe that.

"Hey wassup, C, it's Rico."

"Rico, my man. What happened? I was on my way to ya crib when I saw the jakes out there. What went down?"

"I'm not sure really, but listen, I need you to put your ear to the street. I smell a setup, and I think that bitch Monica had a lot to do with it. The cops ran up in my shit too easily, and I haven't heard shit from her since. I had one of my peeps check for her number, but she's not in the system."

"Yo, Rico, I'm on it, man. Hold your head up in there, man. I'll get back to you soon. Juan still in there?"

"Yeah, he still here, just send word and quickly. I need to know if her ass should be murked or not."

"I'm on it. Hasta la muerte, que exista honor."

"Till death, get at me soon."

* * *

I believed every word Arturo said because that was exactly how it went down. Now all I had to do was get him to take me to the connect and he could be done with. I was considering sparing his life, but I wasn't sure yet. After all, he just did what the boss told him to do, but now he needed to understand that there was a new sheriff in town, and things were about to change.

"So, where is the connect?"

"In D.C., right outside the White House. He works for the President. His coke is flown directly to him without any interruptions. The staff says nothing. It's like everyone is in on it."

"Arturo, this is what I'm going to do for you. If you are willing to work with me I'll spare your life. Understood?"

All he could do was nod. He was badly beaten, and I knew a good sleep would do him justice. I walked over and stood directly in front of him so he could see that I meant business. Hector and Jesus completed the circle around him. We all looked at each other before I spoke again.

"OK, Hector and Jesus will take you to the hospital. I will give you a few days to get yourself together. Come see me Friday morning. We'll go see the connect and get down to business. Understood?"

"Understood."

"Oh, and Arturo, I have the world watching you right now. Don't try to skip town or you really will end up missing."

I left while Hector and Jesus cleaned Arturo up to take him to the hospital. I wasn't really concerned about him running off. He didn't want the dogs on him. I drove around the block a couple of times, stopping to talk to a few of my workers to ensure that an eye was kept on Arturo, then I made my way over to Yolanda's house. She was supposed to get information for me from Monica, and since I hadn't heard a peep from her, I took it as she wasn't moving until I came up off that shopping spree.

Turning my car toward South Philadelphia, I got to Yoyo's house a half hour later. I didn't call beforehand, so I was hoping she wasn't in there with some nut-ass nigga. I didn't feel like bustin' a cap in someone's ass, but I would if I had to. These Tasker niggas thought they had shit on lock, and they hated when I came down this way, but they knew they could get it, and they ain't want that kind of heat. Yet and still, there's always a busta who wants to try you, you know?

Checking my hip to make sure my heat was secure, I parked my car in front of Yoyo's apartment and moved to her door swiftly, looking over my shoulder on the way up the path. No telling who was watching. Even your own will do you in. I knocked on her door like I was the police, and turned my back to it just in case someone tried to walk up on me. Since Rico's demise, fools had been testing me.

"Who is it knocking on my door like the damn police?" Yolanda yelled from the other side of the door, obviously upset. I didn't give a fuck.

"It's C-Dogg, mami. Open the door."

I heard some movement on the other side, and a few minutes later she came to the door dressed in a cut off tank top and boy shorts. My mouth dropped open at the sight of her ass bouncing as she made her way back to the couch. Yoyo had a lot of legs, and I wanted to dive between them.

"Carlos, when did you start popping up unexpected? Did you lose your phone or break your finger?" Yolanda knew she looked good, and I could tell from the look on her face that she was really feeling herself. Her hair was laid, so she must have just gotten it done. And the polish on her fingers and toes looked fresh. I acted like I didn't notice either as I took a seat on the couch across from her and turned up the television.

"It's nothing like that, ma. I was just wondering what was up with you since I haven't heard anything from you in a while. Did you get that information I asked for?"

"That would be no."

"Why not? Yoyo, you know how important this is to me."

"Did you come up off that shopping spree? I think not, because I don't see any new boots in my closet."

"Come on now, mami. You know it's never that serious with me coming up off a few thousand dollars. I just need to know that you're going to ride for me, that's all."

"You know I'll ride for you, C. I just don't think I feel the same love coming from your end."

"Yolanda, you're killing me. Tell me, what I need to do to make this happen. Tell papi what to do."

"Take me to get those Manolo boots I saw, and maybe we can talk."

"Damn, Yoyo, is it like that?"

"Oh, it's like that."

"OK, listen to me. We can go out right now if you'd like. I just need you to call your sister."

"You know damn well by the time I get dressed and make a call the malls will be closed, and you ain't taking me all the way to New York on a Tuesday night, and you ain't fuckin', so no."

I got up off the couch and walked over to her, dropping to my knees in front of her. She kept eye contact, refusing to be the first to turn away. She was looking good. Her lips were all shined up the way I liked them, and her nipples stood at attention through her cutoff tank top, the skin on her belly was smooth like a baby's ass. Forcing myself to stay focused, I made my eyes connect with her eyes and tried to talk to her sensibly. I could definitely see myself making Yoyo a steady, but she had to clean herself up. I couldn't have her around me, knowing she was liable to sniff up half a brick at any given moment.

"Yolanda, listen to what I'm saying. If you call your sister right now and see what's up, I'll take you anywhere you want to go this week. We can leave in the morning, but we have to be back by Friday. I have some things I need to take care of."

"So, what will you do for me right now?"

I said nothing. I just simply moved the crotch of her panties to the side and began making my acquaintance with her clit. I had to hold her down by her legs to keep her still after she eventually took one of her legs out of her panties. I had Yolanda's legs trapped under me so she couldn't move, and she was trying hard to get away. Switching between sucking on her clit and pushing my tongue in and out of her she was losing her damn mind. She begged for the dick, but I refused to give it to her. I needed her to handle business for me, and she could get broke off after that. A half hour later she was on the phone with Monica getting the scoop.

"Listen, before I dial her number I need you to promise me one thing."

"What now, Yoyo?" I asked her while I washed her essence off my face. She was a wet one.

"I know Monica has probably gotten into some shit she had no business being in, but you have to promise me one thing."

"What is it already, damn!"

"You have to promise me you won't hurt her. She's pregnant with my niece or nephew, and she needs to be here for her child. I don't want him or her to go through what Monica and I went through as kids."

"You have my word. I just need her to give me some info on Rico; then I'll call all the dogs off, even Shaneka."

"What beef Shaneka got with my sister? Yo, I know she don't want none. That bitch ain't as crazy as she thinks she is."

"Calm down. She thinks Monica is carrying Rico's baby, that's all."

"OK, but I already told you she's not, so make her aware of the situation before I have to."

"Yoyo, you have my word. Shaneka will not be a problem. Just call your sister, please."

She looked at me like she was leery, but after I started counting out hundred-dollar bills on the countertop, she slowly began dialing the numbers to her sister's residence. Yoyo was really taking me through it this time, but I had to do what I had to do.

"Hey, Monica, how's my little niece or nephew doing?"

I couldn't hear what Monica was saying to her on the other end of the phone, so I just sat back and tried to read Yoyo's facial expressions. I listened as they chatted about baby shit and some kind of mural that Monica had completed for the baby's room. They talked about baby furniture and all that jazz. Monica must have promised her something because she started smiling. I started taking back hundreds, making her face frown up. She gestured for me to hold up.

"So, did you hear more about Rico?"

I wasn't sure what Monica said, but I knew it wasn't good when Yolanda's face frowned up. I wasn't in the mood for no bullshit until I heard Yolanda tell Monica to grab her cell phone and call the ambulance.

"Don't worry, sweetie. Your water just broke. I'll hold on. Just call 911 so someone can come get you. I promise I won't hang up."

For the next twenty minutes I listened to Yolanda as she coached Monica. This bitch was about to have a baby, and I needed some information from her. I'd be calling Tony the locksmith sooner than expected. I wouldn't ransack her house, but I would be paying it a visit very soon.

Monica

Nobody Has to Know

As I felt the pain of the contractions I wondered if the pain I was enduring was worth it. I had been in labor for ten hours now. Yep, I was getting ready to deliver the baby James and I had conceived, and the physical pain from the contractions was almost so unbearable that I began to wonder whether or not getting pregnant by James in the first place had been worth it. While I contemplated my present plight, my mind began to drift back to the emotional pain I had endured during my childhood and adolescent years. I didn't know which pain had been worse, but while the physical pain would eventually end, it seemed I would forever be plagued by emotional pain. Of all times, why during labor was I thinking about my dirty-old-no-good uncle? I could still hear his voice.

* * *

"Monica, open this damn door! What I tell you about locking my damn doors around here?"

I was on the other side, fearing for my life as I hurriedly dressed before my drunk uncle broke down the door. I didn't want him to see me undressed, especially knowing what would happen if he did. I zipped up my pants and tucked my shirt in tightly. I unlocked the door and opened it just before he was about to kick it down.

"Who you got in this room, girl? Who you tryna hide?" Uncle Darryl said, barging into the room and almost knocking me into the wall.

I stood as far away from the bed as possible, not wanting to give him any ideas. I didn't know how I ended up in this never- ending nightmare, but I knew that when I got old enough I would leave. In my heart I vowed that no man would ever touch me once I escaped. Not like this.

"I was 'sleep and didn't hear the door," I replied in a barely audible voice. I didn't want to upset my uncle anymore than he already was.

"Let me find out you lying," he responded with a snarl, "Ain't nobody hittin' that but me, and as ugly as you is won't nobody want cha anyways. Get cha ass downstairs and clean that kitchen. I told you I wanted that done before I came home from work."

"OK, Uncle Darryl, I'm right behind you," I stated, looking around the room for something to do so I wouldn't have to walk past him.

"I said I want it done now. Move ya ass!"

Hesitantly, I moved by him as quickly as I could, almost running. I wasn't fast enough because he reached out, grabbed my pants pocket, and pulled me back by my shirt collar. He reached into my shirt and fondled my young breasts. I grimaced as he rubbed himself against me and kissed behind my ear. I did everything I could to hold back the tears, hoping he wouldn't make me go back into the room.

"Nobody betta not be hittin' this but me. Ya hear?" he whispered into my ear as he continued to explore my under-developed body.

"Yes sir," was my only reply as I made my way downstairs after he released me.

For the life of me, I couldn't figure out what a grown man could see in me. Boys my age thought I was hideous, so I couldn't understand why I had to practically beat my uncle off me at least five nights a week. He seemed to get off on just rubbing the head against me. I gagged every time. I knew the slimy stuff he left behind was not supposed to be there, and I honestly thought the only reason he didn't actually do it to me was because it wouldn't fit.

I found myself on a few nights holding a mirror between my legs so I could look at myself to see if something was different. There was barely any hair there, and it didn't look appealing. But that didn't seem to keep his mouth off it. Uncle Darryl had threatened to kill me if anyone found out, and my fourteen-year-old mind believed it, so I took the abuse, hoping he would die or leave me alone. Who could I tell anyway?

I didn't know what to do about the red bumps that hurt like hell when I went to pee, but I knew I had to do something soon because I couldn't take the itching and burning anymore.

I cried. I wished my mom were still alive. My mother was killed by her lover and I was powerless to help her. My feet felt like lead, like they were glued to the floor. I watched my stepfather beat my mother to death.

When the cops came that day, my sister, the baby of the family, was taken to go live with her Aunt Joyce over in West Philly. My brother, the middle child, was taken to his grandparent's house, and I was stuck with drunk ass Uncle Darryl. I didn't know if I was going to make it out alive, but I knew if I did, every man would pay dearly for what I went through. I thought the abuse would be over when my mom passed away. At least then I wouldn't have to worry about my stepfather trying to sneak into the room late at night, and my mom acting like she didn't know. But I jumped out of the frying pan and into a big ass fire. Uncle Darryl was bold, and the fight was no longer easy. He would pay when the time was right. He and every man after him would get what they deserved.

* * *

A sharp pain in my side quickly brought me back to reality, and soon after my son was born. The doctor said it was too late to give me an epidural, so I had to bear the pain of childbirth. When he came out I didn't want to hold him. The nurse cleaned him up and put him in a crib next to my bed. I was upset that I couldn't take a shower right away. My legs felt like wet spaghetti, so even if I wanted to get out of the bed, I couldn't.

My first instinct was to leave my son in the hospital and let them deal with it. But my heart wouldn't let me. For two days straight I stared at him, letting the nurses feed and change him. I refused to hold him, but I had the nerve to get an attitude because the doctor made him cry during his circumcision. He looked so much like James and Jazz's son Jalil that it wasn't funny. I knew James didn't care, but I decided to call him anyway to let him know his child was born.

It was nearly three in the afternoon, so I called James's job. I was going to take the sucker way out and leave a message on the stations answering machine, but at this point I just felt betrayed. It wasn't really about me anymore. It was about his child. I felt that I needed to talk to James for my son's sake. I dialed the station. The phone rang twice before the nosey old lady who sits at the front desk answered.

"Good afternoon, and thank you for calling The Urban News Network. How may I direct your call?'

"Can you connect me to James Cinque, please?"

"Who may I tell him is calling?"

"His new baby's mother, bitch! Just connect us. Damn all the questions."

The line got quiet for a second, and I thought she hung

up on me. Just as I was about to snap the fuck out I heard James's voice come from the other line."

"Thanks for calling T.U.N.N. This is James speaking. How can I help you?"

"I had a boy."

"Excuse me? Who is this?"

"James, don't play stupid. It's Monica. I had your son two days ago."

It got quiet on the other line, and if it weren't for his breathing I would've thought he had hung up the phone. A part of me felt bad for James. I knew this baby was the last thing he wanted, but this was the consequence of having sex without protection. In the beginning he came to me willingly. It wasn't until later on that he decided to fall back, and that wasn't working too well with me.

"Hello? James, are you still there?" I had a slight smile on my face from his discomfort, but it really wasn't a funny situation. James could shell out all the money in the world. At the end of the day I was the one stuck with a crying baby. I would definitely be getting a live-in nanny. I didn't do diapers.

"Monica, what hospital are you in?"

"The University of Penn. Why, are you coming to see your newborn son?"

"No, I'm coming to get a blood test. This ain't no Jerry Springer shit, OK? I'll be there within the hour."

He didn't give me a chance to say anything else. He just hung up the phone. I placed the receiver back on the base and sat up on the side of the bed to look at the baby up close. They had finally let me shower, so I was able to move around a bit.

I carefully took him out the crib and cradled him to my chest so I wouldn't drop him. There was no doubt in my mind that this was James's son. He had his eyes and everything. Tears gathered at the corners of my eyes, but I refused to let them drop. If I was going to move on to a normal life I had to stay strong.

I laid the baby on my chest and rubbed his back. I giggled as I watched him suck his thumb. It then hit me that there was no turning back. I was a mother. I stared at him for what felt like an eternity. I had no idea how much time had elapsed, but when I looked up and saw James standing in the doorway I knew it was time to face reality, and there was no turning back. It was time to take care of business.

James

Here and Now

I look in your eyes, and there I see what happiness really means. The love that we share makes life so sweet. Together we'll always be...

I stood outside the door and watched Monica and our son for a few minutes before I walked in. I say "our" son, because deep down inside I knew he was mine. Yeah, I truly believed that Monica was a slut, but why lie about something like this?

When I walked into the room she looked at me like she was shocked I had shown up. I stopped at the gift shop before I came up to the room and got her a few "It's A Boy" balloons, and flowers for the side table. I wasn't sure why I made the effort, but she looked appreciative.

I stood at the door for a few minutes, capturing the moment in my mind. Inching closer I slowly made my way to the side of the bed, looking at my son for the first time. Damn, there was no denying him. We had the same face. He looked just like Jalil when he was first born. I blinked back tears, keeping the reason why I was there at the forefront of my mind.

"So, do you believe me now?"

"Monica, I never said I didn't believe you. Any man would have doubts in this situation. Look at the circumstances."

"Fuck circumstances, James. Look at him! This is your child."

Monica began to cry and it was breaking me down. I almost gave in, but I thought about how I got here in the first place. Plus, I needed to come correct with Jazz. Her stomach was growing more every day with our children, and it was only fair to her that we knew how to proceed from here on out. I was a lot of things, but a deadbeat dad wasn't one of them. No, I didn't want Monica in my life, but we had a child together, so I had to do what was needed to make things right.

"Monica, can you buzz the nurse in for the blood test? We need to get this done."

"Blood test? Are you telling me that you are still going to go through with it even though it is clear that James, Jr. is yours?"

"James, Jr.?"

"Yes, James will be a junior. He might as well carry on the family name."

"Monica, Jazz is going to make our son a junior if she has one. You have to change his name."

"It's first come first served in this game. She's just going to have to think of something else."

"Look, Monica . . ."

Monica cut me off as she stated, "You come up in here talking about a blood test and all this other bullshit but what you need to do is bring that blood test shit to your wife because she's probably not even pregnant with your fucking baby!"

Monica was a sick, twisted, manipulative bitch and this was a perfect example of her bipolar ways. But I wasn't trying to fall for her tricks. I knew that those babies Jazz was carrying were my kids. There was no way in hell Jazz would have stepped out on me and gotten pregnant! So I quickly dismissed what Monica had said.

"Look! Call the damn nurse in so we can get this over with. I have to get home to my wife and kids."

Monica paused and looked at me and shook her head.

"So, you're going to go through with this?"

"Either you push the damn button, or I go get her. It's your choice."

As Monica went to her bed to push the button, I walked across the room and leaned my head against the window, trying to think of a way to propel myself into the rush hour traffic that crowded the street fourteen stories down. For a brief second I wondered if my dad was like this and my mom never said anything. Did I have brothers and sisters out there who I didn't know about? How was I going to explain this to Jaden and Jalil? How do I tell them that they have a brother and it's not from their mom?

I took a seat until the nurse came, making myself as comfortable as possible given the situation. Periodically I would look over at Monica. She put Junior back in the crib and was looking at television. The curiosity was killing me. I had to hold him.

I tiptoed over to him and leaned over to get a good look at his face. Gently picking him up and holding him close to my chest, my heart soared when he reached up and wrapped his hand around my pinky finger. The last time I felt like this was when the twins were born, and I almost forgot how it felt to be surrounded by innocence.

Taking my seat again, I studied his face for signs of another man, but it was like I was looking into the fountain of youth. The nurse came in to let us know that she would be ready for us in a few minutes. As she was walking out the room a very stunning woman walked in. She was gorgeous, and my man began to rise to the occasion.

"Girl, you look good considering you just pushed out a baby! Where is my darling nephew?" Still in shock, I stared at the woman who was obviously Monica's sister. She was the bomb, and I had to remind myself that I had a wife at home.

"His father is holding him, but he'll be leaving soon so

you can hold him then. We're waiting on the nurse to come back so she can do the blood test."

"Blood test? For what? Didn't you just say he was claiming him?"

"Yeah, but he has to explain it to his wife, I guess."

"His wife! Monica, are you serious?"

"First of all, you two aren't going to talk about me like I'm not here. If you have any questions about me, or my family, ask me. I have nothing to hide. Monica was a terrible mistake."

I definitely had an attitude. How did they think they were going to put me on Front Street, like this entire episode was my fault? Monica played just as much of a role as I did. I wanted this portion of my life to be over.

Before Monica or her sister could get in another word, the nurse came in to draw blood for the test. I kept my mouth shut and my eyes on Monica while the nurse tried her best to find a vein. She poked me seven times before she was able to draw blood, reminding me why I hated needles. My heart dropped when she went through the hassle with my son, his small cry echoing in my head long after she put a bandage on him

"Sir, if you'd like to wait around, the test should be back from the lab within the hour. It doesn't normally take long."

"That's fine, I'll wait."

The nurse walked out, and I took my seat back in the corner. Monica and her sister made a fuss over the baby, and I heard mention of a shopping spree, but decided not to comment.

In a little over an hour the nurse came back with the results. I wasn't sure I wanted to know. A part of me was hoping he belonged to someone else, but another part of me was hoping he was mine. When I held his little body in my arms, it felt right. The nurse gave both me and Monica a copy of the lab results. I couldn't read mine. I was too scared.

"Monica, I have to get going. We'll talk another time."

"James, what are you talking about? Read the damn paper. This is what you wanted, right?"

"I'll read it later. I just need to get some air right now."

"Let me find out you fuckin' with a deadbeat, Moni. For all this trouble you could've stuck it out with Rico," Monica's sister said from the sideline. I wanted to reach over and pop her in her smart ass mouth, but I decided to just keep it moving. It didn't make sense to cause a scene with my son in the room.

"Monica, when will you be released? Do you have a ride home?"

"I'll be discharged tomorrow. Why, are you coming to get me?"

"I was, but since you have so much to say you can find a way home. I'll be contacting you shortly to let you know what I've decided concerning the baby."

"How do you know he's yours if you won't even read the damn results?"

"I'll talk to you soon."

"Of course you will. You know what's best for you."

Reserving any comment, I left the room and went to sit in my car for a second. It took me twenty minutes and tons of tears before I unfolded the paper from Quest Diagnostics. It stated that Junior belonged to me—99.9 percent certain. Now all I had to do was break the news to Jazz.

On the way home I rode in silence, trying to decide my approach. She was due soon, too. I didn't need her stressing, but I believed that if I didn't tell her now, it would hurt her more later. I had enough with the lies, so I decided I would come straight out with it.

I got home at around five thirty. Jazz was in the kitchen cooking dinner, and the kids were at the table coloring on construction paper. I walked into the kitchen, and after kissing everyone on the cheek, I asked her to follow me out to the patio. She turned the fire on low and walked out behind me, making sure the kids were OK. I didn't say anything. I just handed her the lab results. She looked at me with teary eyes and rubbed her stomach. I was at a loss for words, and waited patiently for her to say something.

"James, what do we do now?"

"We live, sweetie. That's all we can do. We'll have to talk to Monica eventually, but right now all we can do is wait."

I pulled my wife closer and held her in my arms as though it would be my last time. Our family was just starting to come together, and now this. But I was confident we would be OK, somehow. God didn't put more on you than you could handle, and even the worst situation wasn't as bad as it could be. We would get through this . . . we had to.

Jasmine

Confessions

I found out from Yoyo that Monica would be in the hospital for at least two days after she had her baby, so the very next day I went to see my man, Sean. He runs a locksmith shop over near Monica, and I knew for sure that every time he made a key for someone, he made one for himself just in case.

I was almost sure he told me a while ago he had keys to Monica's crib, because he had been hitting her off for a while before she started fooling with Rico. Arturo would be getting out of the hospital in a day or so, so if I was going to do something I had to make it quick. I broke Yoyo off already because she wouldn't shut the fuck up about it, but she knew she owed me some info so I'd get with her later.

My boys told me they saw Monica and Stenton having lunch in the city and they looked like they were in a heavy debate. That scandalous bitch was probably trying to get some dick, with her ignorant ass.

I parked my car on the little island across the street from the shop, just in case I had to make a quick getaway from the Feds, who seemed to constantly be on my back. I checked my surroundings in my mirrors before exiting my vehicle, making a quick exit and practically running across the street. I looked behind me once more before entering the shop.

"Yo, Sean. What's up, my nigga?" We exchanged hand-shakes across the desk.

"Nothing much, man. Just making this money. What brings you to the 'hood today?"

"I came to holler at you about getting a key."

"Say word? To your crib?"

"Now you know I know how you get down, man. You'll never have that much access to my shit." I laughed. I'd hate to put a bullet in his peanut head if my shit ever came up missing.

"So, what can I do for you, man? You know I got the business."

"And that's why I fuck with you. You remember that chick you was hitting over there on Lincoln Drive? The jawn that be having everybody sprung. She was messing with my boy Rico before he got set up."

"Oh, you're talking about Monica. You trying to get at that? The shot is fantabulous."

"Nah. Yo, you a wild boy." I had to laugh to myself because you just never knew what to expect Sean to say. He hit nearly every dame that came through those doors, and I ain't mad at him. A brother got to pay his rent somehow.

"You sure? I can set that up for you."

"Man, I am positive. What I need is access to her crib, if you get my drift."

"Oh, you want me to do some illegal shit."

"Nigga," I had to step back and look at him for a second. I couldn't believe the shit that had just come out of his mouth. "You already doing illegal shit. I'm sure keeping a copy of everyone's keys can't be lawful, right?"

"OK, you got me on that one. I feel you, but that comes at a price."

"Name it, but I need them today."

"You can have all three keys and the pass code to her alarm within minutes for five thousand a pop."

"You telling me you want twenty thousand for me to get in the crib?"

"Cash money up front. And keep my name out ya mouth. I don't need the jakes coming down on my shit. I got a family to provide for."

"Damn, you straight robbing me with my eyes open on that one, Sean. Who you know carry around that kind of money?"

"That's none of my concern. I just need five thousand to get started, and you pay by the key. Do we have a deal?"

"Hold on, man, let me go to my car." I was pissed that this dude was straight raping me for the keys to Monica's house, but that was a small price to pay to get some dirt on her and Stenton and to get him off my ass.

I checked the perimeter and made a mad dash to my car, pushing a few buttons once I got inside to slide out my secret compartment. To the average eye my sound system looked like a basic six disk CD changer, but after pushing a sequence of buttons, the headrest of the passenger seat laid flat, and an entire arsenal slid forward. In the drawer at the bottom I kept a nice stash, but it wasn't anywhere near twenty Gs. Taking the eight thousand I had, I made sure everything was back in order before I stuffed the cash in an old McDonald's bag from the backseat and dashed back across the street. I got a little paranoid when I saw a cop car pull up behind me, but my heart returned to a regular pace when they kept going.

"Look, I don't have twenty thousand on me, but I do have eight. I'll send one of my men down here with the rest of the money in the morning. My word is my bond."

"Your word, huh? Well, just to make it even let me get a copy of the key for your safe house over there on Eighth Street. You know, just for my own safety."

"You have got to be kidding me. Sean, is it like that?"

"Carlos, you know me and you go back like four flats on a Cadillac, but I got to protect my business. It's nothing personal toward you, but I got kids to feed. You do understand, right? Eight thousand is only paying for one and a half keys, and if my black ass gets locked up my family needs to be on point."

"Damn, you are killing me here. Look, how 'bout I give you . . . " I started digging in my pockets for cash, and only came up with a thousand more. If I hadn't given Yolanda that money I would have had at least ten thousand to give him up front.

"This is all I got, man. Just tell me where to meet you later today, and I'll have one of my boys bring you what I owe, plus a little extra for your troubles. It doesn't get any better than that."

"Look, I don't be doing no favors and shit, but I'll do it for you this one time. Next time come correct or step."

"OK, Sean. I feel you. You the man today."

I stood by while Sean counted his money, afterward tucking it safely away in a safe under the desk. I made sure to peep the location on the low just in case I ever had to come back and get this nigga. Ten minutes later I was out the door with three keys and the password to the alarm in my right pocket. I called Hector and told him to send the dough over to Sean, and for him and Jesus to meet me at Monica's crib in an hour. This chick needed to know who she was fucking with. This wasn't a game.

Within the hour we pulled up on Monica's block, opting to park down the street from her house just in case one of her nosey-ass neighbors stayed home from work and was watching her house. With our baseball caps pulled low over our faces, we walked slowly up to her crib like we lived there, and let ourselves in. I was mad after we finally got in because her alarm wasn't even on. That was money I didn't have to spend.

Now, I have to say, her crib was laid. All the pink got under my skin, but she had her shit on point. We took our time looking around the crib just to see if something would jump out at us that we could use. We didn't know exactly what we were looking for.

"Yo, C Dogg! Hector! Come up here. You guys got to see this."

Both me and Hector ran up the steps to see what Jesus had found. We found him in what I assumed to be the master bedroom. Entering the room, I turned my attention to the television to see what all the hoopla was about. That shit on the screen made me want to fuck just walking in there and seeing Monica's naked body.

Apparently, little Miss Monica was very busy. The recording was on fast forward but I could see that Monica was a beast when it came to sex. She had just about everyone in town who was of any importance in a compromising position on that tape. No wonder she walked around like she had shit on lock. She was able to fuck up the lives of politicians, judges, and dudes on the police force. I just shook my head and stopped the tape. I popped it out of the VCR and stuffed it in my inside jacket pocket for later use. I was sure it would come in handy later.

We looked around a little more, just to see what was what. But all I saw were some jewels I didn't need, and a couple of dollars on the dresser. A drawer full of dildos made all of us take a step back. I decided I had what I needed, so we bounced.

On the way back down the street Shaneka and this fly ass chick pulled up to me. Even if I wanted to, I couldn't have kept on walking, because Shaneka would have caused a scene and that was the last thing I needed. I told Hector and Jesus that I would meet them at the car. Stooping down so we were face to face, I paid respect to the driver, then asked Shaneka what was up.

"What you doing around this way? I'm shocked to see you outside of West Philly."

"I had to come check on a few things. What you up to?"

"We about to go see what Monica is up to. I heard she had the baby, but I'm not sure if she's home yet. She got an ass whipping coming to her."

"She ain't home yet. Yoyo told me she just had the baby yesterday. That baby ain't Rico's. It's by some married dude she was fucking with."

"How you know all that?"

"Didn't I just tell you I was talking to her sister?"

"Well, Tanya still owe her, so it's a done deal. I'm on my way through the window."

"Now, Shankea, let's not get stupid. You don't think her neighbors are watching? The moment you climb through that window the cops are called. Here, I got one better for you."

"Carlos, you act like shit is sweet. I owe that bitch. She set up my man."

"Girl, calm the fuck down. She just put him in a bad position. Rico was going to get it regardless. It was just a matter of time."

"Look, I really don't need to hear this right now, Carlos," she said through the window with tears streaming down her face. For the first time I could honestly see that Shaneka did care about Rico. Yeah, she did him dirty, but the love was there.

"Look, here are her house keys, and the alarm is off. I got them from . . . well, that's not important. Go get your shit off, but make it quick. I'm sure someone has seen us coming and going by now."

"Thanks, C Dogg. I owe you one."

"Don't mention it. Just be safe."

Feeling like my work was done, I met up with my boys at the corner and we jetted. I had to make a couple copies of the tape while it was fresh on my mind. I had a feeling life was going to be cool from here on out. I had a couple of officials I needed to see about some things.

Jasmine

Confessions

Tanya and I pulled up in Monica's driveway, not giving a damn who saw us. After fumbling with the locks we finally got in and started tearing the place up. I snatched all the paintings off the walls, afterward cutting them to shreds with a knife from the kitchen. Tanya found cans of paint in what looked like the baby's room upstairs. She started to wreck the mural, but I talked her out of it. That would be the one room we didn't touch. Instead we took the paint and splashed it all over the house, ruining the carpets and drapes. Tanya cut up the couches and chairs. For a second I felt bad for Monica because I knew this shit cost her a grip. Her house was laid like you wouldn't believe, but by the time we got done you would have thought we had a frat party in there.

Tanya took a can of spray paint and painted obscenities all over the walls. After a while I took a seat in the corner and watched her work. It was obvious she had some shit to get off her chest, so I let her handle her business. Before we left I ran to the car and grabbed the baby doll from the backseat.

Going back into the nursery I folded the cover down in

the crib and sat the baby doll under it like it was a real child. On the way up I got the biggest knife I could find out of the kitchen and used it to stab a whole straight through the doll, impaling it to the crib. Then I took some of the red paint that was left over and poured it on the doll, giving it the appearance that it was bleeding. I would never kill her child, but that was a hell of a message to leave behind. After bashing in the television screens I was finally able to pull Tanya away from the house. Our work was done.

Monica

Home Sweet Home?

Sheila came to the hospital to see the baby a few hours before I was to be released. We didn't really have anything to say to each other after the restaurant incident. I said nothing to her the entire time. She held the baby for a second, and after she commented that the baby looked like James, I called security to make her ass leave. Like I needed the constant reminder.

Surprisingly, my sister kept her promise and was at the hospital to take me home. I was so nervous about leaving because I knew once I got home it was all on me. There wouldn't be any nurses to take the child when I didn't feel like being bothered. I knew for sure the first thing I would do was start interviewing nannies. I didn't have the time to be getting my nails messed up changing nasty diapers.

When I pulled up on my block there were several police cars around my house. I started to panic. Did I accidentally leave the stove or the iron on in my haste to leave the house? Or did someone break into my shit while I was gone? Damn, I was only gone for a few days.

I didn't see any flames or fire trucks, so it was safe to assume my shit wasn't burning. The amount of cops on the premises made me nervous. I was clueless as to what was going on. The first officer I recognized was Officer Hill. I approached him after Yolanda stopped the car. I needed answers now.

"Can someone tell me what's going on here?" There had to be at least thirty cops on my property. Some were standing around talking, others were bringing out pieces of my furniture. For the first time in my life I was scared to death.

"Are you the owner of this house?" Officer Hill asked as though he didn't know who I was. I decided to play along until I knew what was going on.

"Yes, I am. What seems to be a problem?"

"One of your neighbors called and reported suspicious activity on the property. She said it might be a possible break in. When we arrived we found your house ransacked. There were no signs of forced entry, so we are assuming the perps had a key. Right now . . ."

I didn't want to hear shit else he had to say. I needed to see for myself what was going on with my house. When I walked in, nothing could have prepared me for what I saw. My house looked like a tornado had blown threw it. My paintings, furniture, everything was torn up. I saw nothing that could be salvaged. I ran through the house like a mad woman, not believing the damage I saw. What broke my heart was what I saw in my son's room.

At first I was happy that whoever did this had spared his room, but what I saw in the crib took my breath away, and all I remember seeing was a bird land on the windowsill before I blacked out. I came to with my sister and half the police force standing over me. All I could do was curl up in a ball and cry.

Officer Hill took the report. They said all they could do was investigate and get back to me. Everyone except Officer Hill cleared out. I couldn't call the judge because all the phone lines were cut, and my cell phone was still in Yolanda's car.

"Well, Monica, we'll be getting back to you with a full investigation. Just thank God you have neighbors who care."

"Thanks for your help. Now can you please leave? I need to get my head together."

"I'm gone, but be careful. Things like this aren't random. I guess your time is up in this town, huh?"

"She said leave, nigga. Damn. What, you don't understand English or something?"

I sat down in a fairly clean corner and tried to understand what had happened. I didn't want to say too much around the cops, but now that they were gone, I could get to the bottom of all this.

Yolanda and I, after finally finding two glasses that weren't broken or chipped, got something to drink. I had her grab the baby and follow me upstairs to my room. I pulled all the ruined linen off so we could sit down, then I grabbed the remote off the side of the bed. After pushing a few buttons, the fake bookshelf on the right wall moved to the side, revealing an entire surveillance system.

"Damn, bitch. You like inch high private eye up in this joint. What the hell do you need with that many TVs?"

"You'll see in a minute. Just let me rewind this tape."

We sat in silence as I began to rewind the tape. Yolanda fed the baby in the process. After the tape stopped, I pushed play and fast-forwarded through the day.

At around five, Carlos and two of his men came in snooping around my spot in search of something. I saw them take a tape out of the VCR after they watched it for a while. Carlos stuck the tape in his top pocket, and they searched around a little more before they left. I never turned the alarm on, but I clearly saw him pull keys out his pocket from the camera I had set up at my door. The tag looked like it came from Sean's shop. I made a mental note to go see him.

After they left, Tanya and the woman I met up at the prison showed up and started tearing up the place. Watching that woman in my son's room and seeing what she did burned me up inside, but I held it down. It didn't make sense to be mad now. Later on in the tape I saw the cops come in. Some of them pocketed my money and jewels. I shook my head in disgust at what was playing out in front of me. Hell, if you couldn't count on the law to have your back, then who could you count on?

Taking the tape from the VCR, I gathered all of my son's clothes into plastic bags, leaving everything I owned minus a few pairs of underclothes and some jeans. There would be a for sale sign out front tomorrow. I would hire someone to come and clean up this mess. Hill was right, I was done with this town.

I stayed with my sister for the time being, giving her a couple thousand for the inconvenience. Carlos acted innocent when he came around, and I told Yoyo not to worry about saying anything to him, just get him for all she could before we left. Within a month's time the house was cleaned out, and all of the damage restored. I left the mural up in the nursery, but painted the rest of the house neutral colors to satisfy the buyer. I was practically giving the house away, so it didn't take any time to get it off the market.

On our last day in Yolanda's apartment I sat alone and contemplated my life. I had to honestly admit to myself that I had caused a lot of the drama, but was I really that bad? Furthermore, did my son deserve to grow up without a fair chance? It didn't take me long to decide, I knew what I had to do.

"Come on, Yolanda. We have a plane to catch, but I have to make one stop first."

"Monica, do you have to do this? Things will be better once we leave here."

"Yoyo, I've already made up my mind. Now let's go. We

have to have the cars over there two hours before lift off, and you know how long the lines get."

I took one last look at my sister's apartment, the place I had called home for the last two months. We would be making a new home in Atlanta, Georgia and I couldn't wait to get there. I had worn Philly out, and there would never be another like me around these parts for a long time.

I took in the city on my ride across town, burning certain landmarks into my mind. I was sad to go, but I knew I had to. There was nothing left here for me except for Jasmine and I had an ace in the hole that I was sure would end her relationship with James if things panned out as I suspected. I had to start over. I deserved a second chance at life and the baby deserved a fair chance at life, and that was what I was determined to provide, all while I waited to reel Jasmine in.

James

The Aftermath

I heard one of the twins crying, so I decided to let Jazz sleep in, and I tended to them myself. Jaden had been having nightmares lately, so I knew it would be a while before I went back to sleep.

As I was coming down the steps I thought I heard someone in my kitchen, and I ran to see what was what. It was three o'clock in the morning, and no one should be downstairs but me. Dashing through the dining room I almost slipped on the hardwood floor as I came to a screeching halt. On my dining room table was a baby in a car seat.

I tiptoed toward the baby, not sure why I was scared. It was only a baby, not a bomb. As I got a closer look, I realized this wasn't just any baby, it was Monica's. I briefly wondered how she got in, but then I saw the note and the house key sitting on the table behind the car seat. Not really knowing what to do, I quickly got the twins a drink before grabbing Monica's child and making my way back upstairs. I made sure the twins drank their water and put them to sleep before I took Monica's baby in to Jazz.

I walked in the room quietly and took the baby out of

the car seat. After grabbing the note I sat down on the bed to gather my thoughts. I looked at the baby for a while, then decided to wake up Jazz. She would know what to do.

"Baby, wake up. I need you to see this."

"See what, James? I gotta get up in a few hours."

"I know, baby, but this can't wait until the morning." When Jazz turned over and opened her eyes, her entire face showed shock.

"James, how the . . . where did . . ."

"She left this note."

Jazz continued to stare at James, Jr. before she began reading the letter out loud. I sat in silence and listened to what Monica had to say.

Jasmine and James,

I know this comes at an awkward moment, but I had no choice. What am I going to do with a baby? For the last two months I tried to be a good mother, but I can't. I fear I'll be just like my mother, and I don't want to take my child through that. I knew if I brought my child to you that he would be where he belonged—with his family.

Jazz, if you don't believe anything else I tell you, believe that I loved you with all my heart. I thought if I had James's baby we could be one. Now I realize it would have never worked. Know that you will always be my woman, but you're James's wife, and I'm cool with that. James, it wasn't all in vain, sweetie. You served your purpose. Take care of your family the way you have been, and know that you will not get any trouble from me in the future.

I gave up total custody of Junior to you and Jazz, and you'll find all of the paperwork in the boxes in your living room. I also returned the house key so you won't have to worry. It's been real. Stay blessed.

Monica

P.S. Jasmine, sweetie don't you think now more than ever is the time to come clean about your little secret rendezvous with the twin brothers from Bally's gym? I mean, word on the street is that they both fucked you in the same bed you and James sleep in! Talk about trifling. At least I had the decency to fuck your husband on the kitchen table and not in the same bed that the two of you sleep on. But to each his own. I think that if you truly love James that you owe it to him to at least tell him the truth. And the truth is you're probably not even pregnant with his kid right now. You know in your heart what I am saying is right. And if I'm wrong then I'm wrong but if I'm right . . . Well . . . James you know about blood tests, so when Jazz delivers why don't you take a blood test to see if what I am saying is wrong? What do you have to lose?

Jazz and I looked at each other with tears in our eyes. I had tears and Jazz had a look of shock in her eyes more than anything else. I walked over to the window in silence, not sure what to think or say but for some sick strange reason I could sense that Monica had actually won in her vindictive selfish war she was waging on the marriage that we were desperately trying to save.

I looked out the window in time to see Monica looking up at me from across the street. Our eyes met briefly before she got into her car and slowly drove away. I didn't know how to feel at that moment. Because although Monica was driving away, I knew that that was only symbolic. She would resurface and I had a deep intuition that when and if she resurfaced that Jazz and I probably wouldn't be together anymore . . .

Epilogue

Monica L. Tyler

I'm rich in love. I'm rich in peace. I'm rich in hope. I'm rich indeed. I'm ready. This is my time. All that I hope for is mine. It's mine, it's mine . . .

I never thought I would leave Philly, but that just goes to show how life can change when you least expect it. Yolanda wasted no time meeting the abundance of men the ATL had to offer. I got her a condo not far from mine so I could keep an eye on her. She was grown, but if I knew Yoyo, she'd be in trouble in no time, and someone had to bail her out, right?

As for me, I was taking it one day at a time. I will say that the first year here I missed my son so much that on a few occasions I packed a bag and was almost on the first thing smoking back to Philly to get him. Each time I got close to the airport or train station I turned my car around at the last minute. I had caused enough pain in James's and Jasmine's lives. I knew my son was in good hands, so there wasn't any need to interrupt a good thing. One day, maybe, we'd meet. I just wondered if I'd recognize him. Would he hate me forever?

It was almost six o'clock. I could finish this painting later. I had an appointment with my therapist and couldn't be late. Dr. Washington has helped me so much since I've been here, and it doesn't hurt that she's easy on the eyes either. But, I'm behaving myself and not going there.

I just wished for the best for my baby, James and Jasmine. Hopefully I would continue on with the therapy and if so I knew that I would be alright.

Plus I had bigger fish to fry. After my appointment I had a date with a certain Philadelphia Eagle who was in town for the weekend, and I didn't want to disappoint him.

I said I wasn't going back to Philly. I didn't say Philly couldn't come to me . . .

Jasmine D. Cinque

I look in the mirror and so much has changed. Ever since I had the babies, I just don't feel the same. Every day I'm working or nursing, not sleeping or eating. And my love life is slipping and I feel to blame. . . .

It seemed like overnight my family grew from three to seven. I've been shocked before, but not like I was when Monica left her child and that fucking note! How do you walk away from your own? But then again who was I to judge her? I needed to be asking myself how could I continue to mislead James into thinking those babies were his?

Nothing is promised to you. You could be a wife today, divorced tomorrow. Your mother could leave and your family could disown you, but your children belonged to you forever. At first I was against Monica's baby being with us, and told James to take the baby to the police, but then I realized that it wasn't just Monica's baby, it was also James's baby, and the second I laid eyes on him I knew he'd be a soft spot in my heart forever. Apparently Monica and her judge friends worked all of the kinks out, because once we signed the papers, James, Jr. was officially our son.

Monica never contacted us, and although we didn't need her money, a check for three thousand dollars came like clockwork every month. Some of it we used to buy him stuff, but most went toward his college fund. I guess that was pretty decent of Monica. After all, she did drop her child off on us.

Not too long after that Janice and Jordan made an entrance into the world, and we'd just been one big, "sometimes" happy, family since then. I'm seeing a therapist because I am determined not to let this depression get the best of me. James has been wonderful through it all, and I couldn't ask for a better husband.

Thank God he never actually pressured me into taking a paternity test. He apparently believed me when I simply dismissed Monica's words in the note as a boldfaced, cunning lie on her part. It tore me up inside to know that she was more than likely right. I reasoned that if I unconditionally loved and accepted the baby that James had fathered with Monica, then that would clear my conscience and it would serve as more than enough reason to have James forever believe that the new set of twins were his, and therefore he would have no choice but to unconditionally love and nurture the lives of the two new babies . . .

James D. Cinque

*And if there's anything I can do, let me know. I promise
you I'll get it done, my pleasure. 'Cause I don't wanna see
you struggling no more . . .*

Life lessons. Some are easier to swallow than others, but
all are worthwhile. If I had it to do all over again I'm sure
there are things I'd do differently. In some respects, I'm glad
I made the mistakes when I did. I've learned that the power
of God is irreplaceable, and no matter how many times you
fall, he'll take you back. He's forgiving, and always has his
eye on you. I've also learned that vows of marriage are not to
be taken lightly, and I cherish every day my wife and I have
together. It's not every day you find your soul mate, and
Jasmine is that in every aspect.

I felt bad when Jasmine suggested we take Junior to the
police, especially when I didn't request a paternity test to see
if what Monica was saying was indeed true. I'm a man, and I
take care of mine. I started going through the baby's things
and I found instructions from Monica to contact a guy
named Judge Stenton and he would take care of everything.
Soon after that the newest additions to our family arrived.
Sheila, surprisingly, helped us. She set Jasmine up with a
wonderful therapist to help her with post-partum depression. She's doing better every day.

I'm steadily climbing the corporate ladder. I keep running into this fly honey from marketing on the elevator, but
every time I think of dipping out, I think of Monica, and my
ass is right back in place. I have a loving wife, wonderful kids,
and a great job. Who could ask for anything more?

Sneak Peek—Coming Soon From Anna J.

GET MONEY CHICKS

A Hustle Gone Dead Wrong

"**B**itch, what is you whispering for? I can't hear a thang you sayin'," my girl Karen yelled into the phone over the loud music in the background.

My heart was beating in my throat, and even if I tried I couldn't speak no louder than I was at the moment. I collected my thoughts as best as I could, but all I could hear were sirens, the clink of handcuffs, and bars shutting behind me. I had to get out of there and quick.

"Girl, you gotta go get Shanna and get over here quick. I think I killed him, girl." By now tears were rolling from the corners of my eyes like a run in a pair of stockings. I couldn't breathe, and my vision was blurring as we spoke.

"Over where? Black Ron's house? I thought you was in there pulling a caper?"

"Karen, listen to me. You have to go get Shanna and come over here now! I need y'all. I don't know what to do."

"No, problem. I think I just saw her pull up to the building. We'll be there in like three minutes."

Instead of responding I hung up. Snatching my clothes from behind the chair, I slid into my gear quickly and went downstairs to wait for my friends. In my heart I hoped this nigga was just playing a cruel joke, and was just trying to scare me. I couldn't go to jail for murder. I didn't have time to be fighting no bitches off me 'cause I was fresh meat, and as sexy as I am there's no doubt they'd be trying to get at me.

Not even four minutes passed, and my girls were pulling up to Black Ron's door. I breathed a temporary sigh of relief as I opened the door to let them in, but the moment the door was closed I busted into tears and fell into Shanna's arms. If my morning didn't start out bad, my night was ending in the worst way.

"Mina, pull yourself together and talk to me. Where is Ron, and what happened?" Shanna said, making me stand up on my own two feet and wipe my face. I sniffled a few times in an attempt to catch my breath. We took seats around the living room, and I ran the entire day down to my girls.

"I met Ron at the club last night and we came here to handle our business. He was already drunker then a mu'fucka so I knew getting ends from him was going to be a piece of cake," I said to them as I wiped snot and tears from my face.

* * *

I went on to tell them how Black Ron, the largest dealer in all of this side of Yeadon, was popping Xani's like they were lifesavers. He had already been drinking way before I saw him at Heat, a local night spot in Sharon Hill over there on Hook Road where all the ballers hung out. He was up in that piece flashing money like he had just won the damn Power Ball, and I was on his ass before any of those other smut bitches could take advantage of his weak state of mind.

We left there around two in the morning, and I ended up having to help him to his car and drive to his crib so he wouldn't kill me and any other unsuspecting motorist behind the wheel. By the time we got to the crib he was able to walk a little straighter, and he made it upstairs just fine.

My plan was to fuck him to sleep and help myself to a little bit of that money when he was out like a light. I would then ask him for money in the morning because I knew he didn't know how much money he was throwing around the night before. I mean, the late great Notorious B.I.G. said it best, "Never get high on your own supply." A chick like me will catch you slippin' and then the next thing you know, it's curtains.

By the time I got finished taking a shower and came back into the bedroom, this nigga was lying back in the bed with his dick in his hand watching *My Baby Got Back* on the television. Silly me thought he would be out for the night, but I guess I would have to work for my money this evening.

"You feeling better?" I asked him, inching closer to the bed. He turned his attention my way for a split second before looking back at the television.

"Yeah, my head pounding a little, but I'm cool. Thanks for seeing that I got home. Out of all the tricks I fuck with, you are the only one I truly trust."

I didn't say anything, instead I toweled my body dry and began to apply some of the lotion he had on his dresser. I pretended not to pay him any mind, but I saw him go from watching me to watching the porn movie out of the corner of my eye. I made a display of massaging my breasts and spreading my legs, acting the entire time like he wasn't in the room.

"Girl, get over here and ride this dick. What you puttin' all that damn lotion on for anyway? You just gonna be ashy in the morning all over again."

I continued to lotion my body like I didn't hear what he said. He was stroking his dick in a long, slow motion, and I'd be damned if I didn't want some of it. Black Ron was definitely working with some shit. I figured I might as well make it a two for one deal. Get the best nut of my life, and the cash to go with it.

Walking over to the bed, I waited until I got to the side to drop the towel. Through half-closed eyelids, Ron watched me give him head while he finger fucked my pussy and smacked me on my ass.

Now, this nigga had been drinking Henney all night, so I knew this was gonna be forever. My head skills were impeccable, and in no time flat I was swallowing all of his babies. But his dick was still standing at attention.

"Damn, girl. If you used your head for anything else you'd be a genius. Get up and ride Daddy's dick."

Ignoring the comment he made, I did what I was told, riding him like I'd been taking horse riding lessons my entire life. I guess my momma's dreams of me being a ballerina were crushed, because the woman I am now is nothing like the girl I was back in the day.

I was on his dick hard, knowing the payout at the end of the night would be marvelous. He stretched my long legs out in all kinds of directions, and I could have sworn I heard him saying something about loving me before he pulled his dick out and busted yet another nut in my face. I pretended like I enjoyed it while he panted all hard in an effort to catch his breath beside me.

Reaching over to the side of the bed, I grabbed the towel to remove his children from my face. This dude was a beast, and although I could see him falling asleep, I knew it would be on again in the morning. I took that moment to take eight one hundred dollar bills from his pants pocket and put it in my wallet before lying in the bed next to him. He snuggled up close to me, and before I knew it I was 'sleep, too.

In the morning I woke up to him sliding his already hard dick into me from the back, and I had to clear the cold out of my eyes so I could focus. This nut was a little quicker than last night, and I was grateful. I laid back in the bed and watched him stumble around the room, and almost fall into the hallway over one of his Timberland boots. I laughed, but not out loud, because Black Ron is crazy and has been known to knock a chick upside the head for less. When he came back into the room, his eyes looked bloodshot, and he damn near crawled to the bed to get in it.

"You gonna be okay, BR?" I asked, noticing his breathing was getting heavier and he was breaking out in a sweat. I didn't know what was wrong with him, but I wouldn't just leave him like this. I still had to get paid for my services.

"Yeah, I'm cool. Those damn pills got me trippin'," he said in a slurred tone as his eyes closed, and his head fell to the side.

"How many did you take?" I asked, scared as hell. I didn't know what was happening, but I couldn't call the cops because I knew this nigga had drugs or something up in this camp, and I'd be damned if I was going to jail for conspiracy.

"Like four of 'em this morning, but I'm cool. I just need to sleep it off."

I didn't answer; I just moved closer to him and let him put his head on my stomach. Not too long after that he was snoring and I was able to turn him on his back. I watched him for a little while, but before I knew it I was asleep, too.

* * *

"And when I woke up he wasn't breathing and was foaming at the mouth. I concluded my story in a loud wail. "Lord, please, if you get me out of this one I promise I'll stop being a hoe!"

"Girl, he prolly just thirsty. Let's go see what's crackin," Karen said, and we all got up and followed her upstairs. When we got into the bedroom, he was the same way I left him: sprawled out on the bed, ass naked, with his dick pointing to the ceiling.

"Damn, that nigga working with that? I had no idea," Karen said as she got closer to the bed. I stayed my ass by the door because I didn't know if he was going to jump up or what.

"Damn girl, I know you said you had a killer pussy, but I didn't know you was for real about that shit," Shanna said.

While Karen and Shanna stood there laughing and high-fiving each other I was a nervous wreck standing in the doorway. I killed a man—I think. And I didn't know what to do. How was I going to get my hot ass out of this mess?

"OK, I gotta plan." Karen's loud-ass mouth brought me out of my trance. At that point I was open to anything, as long as no one pointed the finger at me.

"OK, what is it?" Shanna said while scoping the room out. I'm sure she was looking for something to take, and I could care less. I just wanted to leave.

"Mina, wash him and dry his body off. Fix the sheets around him when you're done. Shanna, go get a trash bag out of the kitchen. It's clean up time."

"I ain't touchin' his dead ass. You do it!" I yelled at her, still stuck in the doorway. I wasn't about to go nowhere near Black Ron. The next time I would see his ass was at his funeral.

"Bitch, that's your pussy juice all over him. You want the feds to come and get your ass?"

I stood there for a second more before I ran to the bathroom to throw up. I couldn't believe the turn my day had taken, and I knew if nothing else I had to walk away clean. Taking the rag from the sink I used the night before, I soaped it up and went to the room to handle my business. It was hard for me to clean up Ron's dead body, but what else could I do?

I didn't want to get caught so I had to handle my business. In the meantime, Karen had found his stash, along with his jewels and a couple of brand new button-down shirts with the tags still on them. We cleaned as best we could and was out of there in no time.

Back at Karen's crib, she counted the money we took from Ron's while Shanna rolled one of five Dutches and I stared out of the window watching the world pass me by. I couldn't believe the life I was living, and I knew after today things had to change.

I got up and changed into a pair of Karen's sweats, taking the club outfit I wore the night before and throwing it in the garbage. I didn't want anything to remind me of that horrible day. I came back in the living room just in time to get the blunt passed to me. Inhaling deeply, I hoped the effects of the illegal drug would cloud my mind long enough for me to make some sense of what happened. I was scared to death, and even though my girls told me I would be cool, I knew I was waiting for what happened to come around to me.

"So, what do we do now?" I asked Karen and Shanna. The weed started to take effect, and I wanted to enjoy my high as long as possible.

"We wait. I'm sure someone will find his body soon. We just act like we don't know nothing and keep it moving. We got a couple of thousand to spend. So we focus on that."

I knew Karen was right, but I couldn't help but think about it. I was now sure that it was the Xanex pills that killed Black Ron, but I was the last one seen with him, and that was my biggest fear. For right now, I would do my best not to worry, but like they always say . . . what you do in the dark always comes out in the light.

About the Author

Taking her first shot at writing a novel, Anna J. is coauthor of *Stories To Excite You*—released during the fall of 2004. *My Woman His Wife* was the first of many full length works of fiction this proclaimed "Diva" will be putting out there for your reading pleasure.

As a full-figured model, Anna is no stranger to being in the spotlight and rather enjoys the attention. Anna is also one of the faces of The Philadelphia Writers Partnership, an editing service for up and coming authors. She resides in Philadelphia and is currently working on her next book.

LOOK FOR MORE HOT TITLES FROM

Q-BORO BOOKS

TALK TO THE HAND - OCTOBER 2006
$14.95
ISBN 0977624765

Nedra Harris, a twenty-three year old business executive, has experienced her share of heartache in her quest to find a soul mate. Just when she's about to give up on love, she runs into Simeon Mathews, a gentleman she met in college years earlier. She remembers his warm smile and charming nature, but soon finds out that Simeon possesses a dark side that will eventually make her life a living hell.

SOMEONE ELSE'S PUDDIN' - DECEMBER 2006
$14.95
ISBN 0977624706

While hairstylist Melody Pullman has no problem keeping clients in her chair, she can't keep her bills paid once her crack-addicted husband Big Steve steps through a revolving door leading in and out of prison. She soon finds what seems to be a sexual and financial solution when she becomes involved with her long-time client's husband, Larry.

THE AFTERMATH
$14.95
ISBN 0977624749

If you thought having a threesome could wreak havoc on a relationship, Monica from My Woman His Wife is back to show you why even the mere thought of a ménage a trios with your spouse and an outsider should never enter your imagination.

THE LAST TEMPTATION - APRIL 2007
$6.99
ISBN 0977733599

The Last Temptation is a multi-layered joy ride through explorations of relationships with Traci Johnson leading the way. She has found the new man of her dreams, the handsome and charming Jordan Styles, and they are anxious to move their relationship to the next level. But unbeknownst to Jordan, someone else is planning Traci's next move: her irresistible ex-boyfriend, Solomon Jackson, who thugged his way back into her heart.

LOOK FOR MORE HOT TITLES FROM

Q-BORO
BOOKS

DOGISM
$6.99
ISBN 0977733505

Lance Thomas is a sexy, young black male who has it all; a high paying blue collar career, a home in Queens, New York, two cars, a son, and a beautiful wife. However, after getting married at a very young age he realizes that he is afflicted with DOGISM, a distorted sexuality that causes men to stray and be unfaithful in their relationships with women.

POISON IVY - NOVEMBER 2006
$14.95
ISBN 0977733521

Ivy Davidson's life has been filled with sorrow. Her father was brutally murdered and she was forced to watch, she faced years of abuse at the hands of those she trusted, and was forced to live apart from the only source of love that she has ever known. Now Ivy stands alone at the crossroads of life staring into the eyes of the man that holds her final choice of life or death in his hands.

HOLY HUSTLER - FEBRUARY 2007
$14.95
ISBN 0977733556

Reverend Ethan Ezekiel Goodlove the Third and his three sons are known for spreading more than just the gospel. The sanctified drama of the Goodloves promises to make us all scream "Hallelujah!"

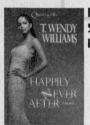

HAPPILY NEVER AFTER - JANUARY 2007
$14.95
ISBN 1933967005

To Family and friends, Dorothy and David Leonard's marriage appears to be one made in heaven. While David is one of Houston's most prominent physicians, Dorothy is a loving and carefree housewife. It seems as if life couldn't be more fabulous for this couple who appear to have it all: wealth, social status, and a loving union. However, looks can be deceiving. What really happens behind closed doors and when the flawless veneer begins to crack?

LOOK FOR MORE HOT TITLES FROM

Q-BORO
BOOKS

OBSESSION 101
$6.99
ISBN 0977733548

After a horrendous trauma. Rashawn Ams is left pregnant and flees town to give birth to her son and repair her life after confiding in her psychiatrist. After her return to her life, her town, and her classroom, she finds herself the target of an intrusive secret admirer who has plans for her.

MICHELLE McGRIFF

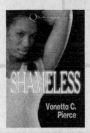

SHAMELESS- OCTOBER 2006
$6.99
ISBN 0977733513

Kyle is sexy, single, and smart; Jasmyn is a hot and sassy drama queen. These two complete opposites find love - or something real close to it - while away at college. Jasmyn is busy wreaking havoc on every man she meets. Kyle, on the other hand, is trying to walk the line between his faith and all the guilty pleasures being thrown his way. When the partying college days end and Jasmyn tests HIV positive, reality sets in.

Vonetta C. Pierce

MISSED OPPORTUNITIES - MARCH 2007
$14.95
ISBN 1933967013

LATONYA Y. WILLIAMS

Missed Opportunities illustrates how true-to-life characters must face the consequences of their poor choices. Was each decision worth the opportune cost? LaTonya Y. Williams delivers yet another account of love, lies, and deceit all wrapped up into one powerful novel.

ONE DEAD PREACHER - MARCH 2007
$14.95
ISBN 1933967021

Smooth operator and security CEO David Price sets out to protect the sexy, smart, and saucy Sugar Owens from her husband, who happens to be a powerful religious leader. Sugar isn't as sweet as she appears, however, and in a twisted turn of events, the preacher man turns up dead and Price becomes the prime suspect.

TONY LINDSAY

Attention Writers:

Writers looking to get their books published can view our submission guidelines by visiting our website at:
www.QBOROBOOKS.com

What we're looking for: Contemporary fiction in the tradition of Darrien Lee, Carl Weber, Anna J. Zane, Mary B. Morrison, Noire, Lolita Files, etc; groundbreaking mainstream contemporary fiction.

We prefer email submissions to: candace@qborobooks.com in MS Word, PDF, or rtf format only. However, if you wish to send the submission via snail mail, you can send it to:

Q-BORO BOOKS Acquisitions Department
165-41A Baisley Blvd., Suite 4. Mall #1
Jamaica, New York 11434

*** By submitting your work to Q-Boro B
Q-Boro books harmless and not liable
works as yours that we may already be cons
in the future. ***

1. Submissions will not be returned.
2. **Do not contact us for status update**
   receiving your full manuscript, we w
   or telephone.
3. Do not submit if the entire manuscr

Due to the heavy volume of submissions, i
not followed, we will not be able to proce